Total-E-Bound Publishing titles from these authors:

By Aliyah Burke

Through the Fire
Seducing Damian

By Jennah Sharpe

Her Handyman
Wish Fulfilled

By SL Majors

Naughty Nibbles: Imagine
Naughty Nibbles: Balls to the Walls

By Bronwyn Green

Celtic Fire: Solstice Seduction
Legend: Moonlight Magic
Brits in Time: Mist and Stone

CAMOUFLAGED HEARTS

A MARRIAGE OF CONVENIENCE
ALIYAH BURKE

IN THE ARMS OF A PILOT
JENNAH SHARPE

DOUBLE TIME
SL MAJORS

FROM THE RUINS
BRONWYN GREEN

CAMOUFLAGED HEARTS ANTHOLOGY
ISBN # 978-1-906590-27-7
A Marriage of Convenience ©Copyright Aliyah Burke 2008
In the Arms of a Pilot ©Copyright Jennah Sharpe 2008
Double Time ©Copyright SL Majors 2008
From the Ruins ©Copyright Bronwyn Green 2008
Cover Art by Anne Cain ©Copyright 2008
Interior text design by Claire Siemaszkiewicz
Total-E-Bound Publishing

A MARRIAGE OF CONVENIENCE

Aliyah Burke

Dedication

To Angie who is watching from Heaven.
Thanks for the wings.

P r o l o g u e

Ayanna Barker moved in time with the fairground's loud music as she stood in line at the beer tent. For a brief moment, the skies were silent as the air show regrouped for the final demonstration which would be followed by a huge fireworks display. So for the time being, it was solely the music that pulsed through her.

Taking a step forward as the line progressed, Ayanna shivered at a light touch on her back. Looking over her shoulder, she met the deep chocolate eyes of the tall, handsome man behind her, and her mouth grew dry.

He towered over her, yet she didn't feel threatened, at least not in a physical way. Sexual...it was way off the charts, he oozed sexual prowess and it was a bit intimidating. A dark grey shirt wrapped his muscled torso and his lower body had been poured into a pair of light blue jeans that had a hole above one knee. As her gaze travelled down, she noticed the grey hiking boots on his feet. Not an inch of him was ignored by her stare; he was just too damn fine.

Moving her eyes back to his, Ayanna was blown away by the primal lust blazing in his gaze. Shoving back a similar reaction, she turned and focused her attention back on the line before her. *That would be a great man to have a fling with. God, my pussy is dripping just from that slight touch. I can't imagine what a night with him would be like.*

Michael Taylor had been talking on his cell phone when he'd stepped into the busy beer tent line. A jostle from behind had almost shoved him into the woman in front of him. His hand had swiped across the bottom of her back and in that second, everything else had faded away. Electrical currents had showered him. The second her soulful brown eyes had landed on his, it was as if he'd just hit mach one in his jet.

He'd stood still as her eyes had travelled hungrily over him. Part of him had wanted to preen while more of him had wanted to lift her up, carry her away from everyone and kiss her senseless. And keep going from there.

What the hell am I thinking? I don't know this woman, but damn if I don't want to.

She wore a purple open-backed shirt that perfectly offset the nutmeg hue of her skin and a pair of hip hugging black jeans. He saw sandals on her feet and if he moved his head just so, he could see the dark purple on her toenails.

While their physical connection was over almost immediately, the ardent impression still lingered between them. He wasn't blind to the desire swirling in her eyes no matter how she tried to pretend indifference.

Paying for her beer along with his, it seemed only natural to settle his large palm against the smooth, dark skin of her back as they left the overcrowded beer tent.

He had no problem following her. The gentle scent on her skin reached out and wound around him, making him yearn for more of her. He craved to find out if her perfume was just around her neck or if the tempting smell went all the way to her feet.

When she stopped to allow a group of people to pass, he leaned forward and murmured, "Michael," into her ear.

Her head turned, positioning her full tempting lips a hairsbreadth from his, and she whispered, "Ayanna."

He kissed her. He had no choice. Her mouth had teased him as it formed her name and challenged him to sample her lips. She tasted divine.

The innocent kiss quickly evolved into something more. Michael hungered for all that this woman offered. He dominated the kiss, using his tongue to sweep throughout the recesses of her mouth.

His cock swelled and dug into her side as Michael plundered her mouth. He groaned his pleasure as the kiss lengthened.

The roar of jets in the sky rumbled around them and put a miniscule distance between their bodies as he struggled for restraint.

Ayanna's lips were swollen from the force of their kiss.

"I want you," he stated bluntly as he watched the rapid rise and fall of her chest. She ran her tongue over her lips.

"Yes," she breathed huskily.

"After the show." Taking her hand, he led her to a vacant spot on the ground. They watched the show like any other couple, holding hands, exchanging kisses, and occasionally staring into each other's eyes. As the park had begun to empty after the show, Michael kept one muscled arm around her, anchoring them together. They'd stopped at the entrance. Pressing her against the cool wall of a ticket booth, Michael ran his hands through her short hair. Strong legs settled on either side of her thin body, eliminating any means of escape.

Courtesy of the night sky his eyes appeared black as obsidian but as gentle as Egyptian cotton.

Ayanna had no intention of going anywhere. This was her night to give in and have a fling. And the man whose breath still held the faint smell of beer was the one her body craved.

"Do you need to tell anyone goodbye?" His voice pulled like crushed velvet over her skin.

"No, my friend saw me with you." Ayanna looked up. "Unless you're leaving alone."

A pleased, yet arrogant grin crossed his face. "Let's go."

The door closed with a click, but the couple embracing barely noticed. Michael and Ayanna's mouths had rarely left one another during the walk from the parking lot to the hotel. Inside the elevator, he'd begun kissing her again, not caring they were in public, being stared at. He had what he desired in his arms.

In the hall, it had taken a passer-by clearing his throat for Michael to remember he hadn't yet reached Ayanna's room. But, he'd hardly slowed in his quest to dominate his lover's mouth. He'd moved his powerful body slightly and effortlessly lifted the woman into his arms, opting to carry her the rest of the way.

Now, as the door to her room shut behind them, Michael reluctantly let the captivating woman in his arms stand on her feet. Both of his hands cupped her face as he lingered at her luscious mouth before slowly drawing away from the nectar he classified as his own ambrosia.

"Do you want a drink?" he asked.

Ayanna stepped closer, eliminating the distance he'd put between them. "No."

"Tell me one thing, Ayanna," Michael ordered as he watched her fingers trail up his arm.

"What?" She never spoke above a whisper.

"Where do you live?"

Ayanna hadn't expected that question. She didn't want to tell him. There was something else she wished from this man, and talk wasn't necessarily high on the list. She wanted one hell of an explosive night of sex with him.

"Around," she hedged as her hands moved from his arms to the hem of his taut shirt. Slowly, she pulled it up, baring the golden-tan planes of his hard chest.

Her body was jerked against his as his mouth covered hers with a ferocity that stunned them both. He was claiming her, branding her, marking her for the rest of their lives.

She shivered as his masculine taste filled each of her senses. Her knees were shaky and her heart beat erratically. At the same time, she felt perfectly safe. This large, powerful man who could snap her in half with his strength made her feel safer than she'd been in her entire life. No other man had ever evoked such powerful and intense reactions in her body, physical or emotional. She shivered as his touch electrified her. Until she had been exposed to *his* intoxicating touch, the idea of actually going through with a one-night stand hadn't been feasible. As Ayanna stared at this walking sex ad, she realised that was *all* she was thinking about.

Wetness pooled between her thighs as she moaned into his mouth. Her teeth grazed the top of the tongue thrusting inside her. Her skin felt like it was being eaten alive with flames. She wanted more. She wanted the hard ridge digging into her belly to slide deep inside her.

Her body bent backwards as Michael continued to plunder her mouth. Each stroke of his tongue brought more wetness to her cleft and she craved more. As he braced her with one arm, his other hand palmed her stomach and inched its way under her ribbed shirt.

His callused hand on her sensitive belly was enough for her internal muscles to clench with longing. She whimpered into his mouth as her grip tightened on his collar.

Thanks to his touch, exhaustion from her emotions plagued her body and there was so much more to come for them in this night.

"Ayanna," Michael crooned into her mouth as his hand moved further up her torso.

He kept his touch light as his fingers danced along her ribs until they met with the cool satin covering the underside of her firm breasts. He skimmed along the tempting globes and her body tensed. Each time she shivered, he felt his cock twitch in response. Slowly bringing her back to a full-standing position, Michael ran his gaze over the enchantress before him. Silken skin the colour of rich nutmeg, brown eyes smoky with passion, full lips, parted and swollen and begging for him to sample again. He couldn't resist her.

He dragged his hands down her sides then back up, bringing along the bottom hem of her shirt. His fingers caressed the skin of her arms as he pulled her top off and dropped it to the floor.

"Jesus," he bit out. His mouth grew dry. She wore a pale lavender sateen bra and the way it complimented her body's natural rich colour made him almost erupt in his jeans. Dropping to his knees before her, Michael pressed feather-light kisses to her bared belly. His hands settled on her hips as his tongue dipped into the depression of her navel.

Her whimper was like a scream of ecstasy to his ears. Every breath he took brought the spicy scent of her arousal to his nose. Michael tightened his fingers on the waistband of her jeans as he fought for control.

He looked at her belly and noticed five freckles forming a circle. He traced them with his tongue as he unbuttoned her pants. Pulling them down her hips and legs, Michael groaned as her matching coloured boy panties were exposed. Tossing her pants to the side, he unfastened the delicate straps of her sandals.

When all she wore was her panty set, Michael stood and looked his fill. Incredible. Stunning. Gorgeous. Sexy as all hell.

The tightness in his pants snapped him from his thoughts.

Ayanna's body prickled with anticipation. Every hair stood on end and each synapse was alive with one identical reaction to the man before her. Wanton desire. Her panties were soaked, and he still wore jeans and hiking boots.

She eagerly explored his lightly haired chest. Her fingers memorised each dip and swell carved into his rock-solid torso. As her nails scraped over his tight nipples and he groaned, a siren's smile crossed her face.

One hand travelled over the large bulge in his pants. Her fingers squeezed lightly as it twitched beneath her touch, and she licked her lips instinctively.

"Keep that up, and we won't be going slow." His deep voice slid over her and sent her to a higher state of arousal.

"You're the one still in boots, handsome." Ayanna dropped her hand to rest on his muscled butt cheek.

He gathered her close and kissed her furiously until her entire body went limp. "Ten secs and they'll be gone."

Eyes still heavy, Ayanna remained immovable as he made short work of his boots, stood and pulled her back into his embrace. Mouths reunited with enough heat to melt the arctic as they stumbled through the dim room to fall on the bed.

Ayanna couldn't remember removing her bra, but the way his mouth suckled upon her breasts made it irrelevant. He nipped, laved and made love to each breast until she thought she'd died. Her body shook from orgasms. She didn't know when one ended and the next began.

His devilish mouth moved between her breasts before trailing down her flat belly. His hands were gentle as they removed her panties. She had no warning as Michael's mouth covered her bald pussy, ran his tongue up the slit and began to feast.

"Ah!" she screamed to the room, her back arching as his tongue flicked mercilessly against her already swollen clit. When she moved he readjusted his body and continued his endless assault. *This man is going to kill me and he's still dressed.*

Heaven. Michael lost his control as her glistening crux was exposed. Her pussy was completely shaved allowing her pleasure to be seen. This whole woman was magnificent. The heady scent that had tantalised him since they'd gotten into the car earlier filled him even more now. He held her wet panties in his hand and before him was a pussy whose swollen clit peeked through the hairless lips. He leaned forward to touch his tongue to her shiny nub then he slid his tongue into her wet heat.

"Oh my God!" Her cry wrapped around him.

His eyes fluttered as her essence filled his mouth. She tasted like spicy candy and he craved it. His cock throbbed painfully as he enjoyed her. He lapped at her thick cream.

Each swipe of his tongue, every suckle of his mouth, pulled a deep throaty cry from the exquisite beauty. He slid his arms under her smooth derriere and held her still so she couldn't writhe away from his touch.

The way her lithe body thrashed, how her cries filled the room, how her hands pressed against the back of his head keeping him where she wanted him... It all made Michael want to dominate, claim, and possess Ayanna until she knew she belonged to him.

"Please Michael," she begged in a faint voice.

He shucked his jeans and boxers. Moving back up her body, he saw the longing in her eyes matched what he felt deep in his soul, a gut-wrenching need to be joined totally with her. Mixed in with the physical desire was something else, something more, an emotion he hadn't experienced with another woman ever.

He picked up the condom packet, opened it and rolled it on his engorged shaft. He counted to gain control when her gaze landed on him and her pink tongue swiped over her lips.

Positioning his body between her spread legs, Michael almost lost his hard-won control when her hand touched his cock and guided it into her wet warmth. As her pussy welcomed him, Michael encountered euphoria and his body thrummed with electricity. Her muscled walls gripped him tightly as he slid fully into her body. The heat almost seared him. Images grew blurry as he sank until he could go no further.

"Fuck me!" he uttered on a harsh breath. The pleasure was almost too much.

"Oh, God!" Ayanna moaned and shuddered as another orgasm took her.

The rippling sensation snapped the tenuous hold Michael had on his control. He began to pump. Back and forth. Her body clutched at him as he withdrew, trying desperately to prevent his leaving, and conformed perfectly to his erection as he moved back inside.

Her panting grew louder as her hips gyrated and move up to meet his thrusts. Michael kissed her as his hips moved faster. Deeper. Harder. Her short nails dug into his back as he continued to pound into her.

"You feel so good, Ayanna," he muttered into her ear as he slid his hands under her shoulders and gripped the back of her head.

"Michael," she mewled.

"Tell me, baby." Sweat covered his body as he tried not to come before she reached her orgasm. Her body tightened around him. *I want to partake of you without a condom on, Ayanna. I want to spill myself deep inside you.*

"I'm...I...I'm..." Her words were garbled. Her actions weren't. Ayanna tightened her legs as her back arched in time with her climax. The waves of pleasure sailing through her propelled Michael over the edge of the cliff he'd been teetering upon. He came with a gravelled shout, his eruption longer than it had ever been before.

Collapsing beside her, he kissed her then disposed of the condom before gathering her back into his arms. They both lay in silence as their hearts slowed and their breathing returned to normal.

He knew they had the night and he wanted to enjoy her luscious body as much as he could. He also realised something else.

Something more meaningful than just sex had happened between them. More powerful than the flames that erupted where they'd touched, the intense experience between them had an undercurrent of destiny. It was almost as if the fates had tipped their hand and brought them together.

Ayanna was boneless and limp. And unsure. This was supposed to just be a good session of sex — which it had been — but her invading emotions threw her. The only thing she was sure of was that she wanted more. More of the pleasure Michael brought her.

His penis hardened against her as his lips moved over her ear. "Take a shower with me."

"Okay," she agreed. *I can't get enough of his touch.*

They walked to the bathroom, heedless of the clothes scattered on the floor of her hotel room. The heat lamp was switched on along with the fan before Michael turned on the water.

When he faced her, her breathing hitched. Goosebumps popped up along her body. His eyes watched her and they looked sleepy, but she knew…she knew they were anything but. Her own gaze moved up and down his hard, naked body. His mouth-wateringly handsome body.

Unbidden, she reached for his fully erect cock and wrapped her fingers around it. His hiss of pleasure reached her, but she ignored it. She focused on what she held.

She swiped her thumb over the tip of the swollen head and it jumped in her palm. In her peripheral vision, Michael's hand clenched. She moved her other hand along the shaft, slipping down to the nest of dark hair at the base and up until it met the one that teased the head of his cock.

Drops of pre-cum were smeared with each pass of her thumb over his hard rod. It was like touching steel covered by warm silk. Ayanna dropped to her knees on the plush bathroom rug and replaced her thumb with her mouth. Her hands shifted down, one on his thick shaft and the other caressing his balls.

"Ayanna!" Michael's voice was hoarse. His rigid posture exposed the tendons of his neck.

Running her tongue under the bulbous head of his cock, Ayanna hummed against him vibrating the tip. But instead of waiting for a reply she moved down the shaft, taking more and more of him into her mouth. She continued to tease his scrotum as her mouth alternated its pressure.

He pumped his hips, driving himself into her while she kept her eyes on his face. His shout announced his release as he came deep in her throat. Before the sound faded, he had pulled her from the floor, kissed her, took her in the shower and proceeded to fuck her like there was no tomorrow.

The water cascading around them only added to the pleasure. The steam made it more exotic. Michael gripped her hips, as she faced him, her back against the wall.

He pulled out of her seconds before he came and spilled his seed onto the dark skin of her belly, only to have it washed away seconds later by the shower. Afterward, she let him carry her back to bed where he loved her all over again.

Every muscle ached, but this man was like a drug. She craved more. It was going to be hard to walk away in the morning.

As she rode him at her own pace, she looked at him again. His eyes spoke of more than just a one-night stand. Neither of them seemed to remember he wasn't wearing a condom. Neither of them seemed to care.

In the morning, however, when Ayanna woke, sore but content, she was alone. There was no sign of Michael Taylor anywhere. Staring at her reflection in the mirror she smiled sadly.

"That's what happens when you agree to a one-night stand."

Chapter One

Michael opened the purse he'd found and searched for some identification so he could have the owner paged. As his tanned fingers slipped through the interior they passed a book of American poets—Edgar Allen Poe, Langston Hughes, Robert Frost, Walt Whitman, and more. He found a container of orange breath mints. A playbill for one of his favourite shows, *The Phantom of the Opera,* was crumpled up on the bottom and under that, he finally found an identification card. He immediately recognised the woman pictured on the Exchange employee card. She worked in the flower shop, but he'd seen her in the bookstore, as well.

Standing, he curled one hand over the muted purple purse and headed for the door. Not even the loud roar of the F-18s and other aircraft flying overhead distracted him from his 'mission'. As a pilot stationed here at Naval Air Station Oceana in Virginia Beach, the sounds were all common place to him.

Crossing the parking lot of NAS Oceana's main Navy Exchange, Michael fought the grin which almost crossed his suntanned face as he watched a few children walk past him in their 'I ♥ Jet Noise' tees. He knew he was receiving strange looks from people as he walked in the Exchange, carrying a purse, with no woman beside him, and for some reason it didn't bother him. Today was a good day.

It was summer in Virginia. Everything was hot, so it was nice to enter the air-conditioned building. He breathed a bit easier without all the humidity in the air. Moving past the beauty salon, barbershop, GNC, and the bookstore, he headed directly to the floral department where he saw the woman he searched for.

"Can I help you?" she asked, coming towards him.

"I believe you dropped this outside, Ma'am."

"Oh, my goodness. I couldn't find it. It must have fallen out of my bag. I've been looking everywhere for my card to swipe, and I didn't..." she trailed off, apparently realising she was rambling. Clearing her throat, she muttered, "Thank you so much...?"

He smiled at her. "Taylor. Lieutenant Michael Taylor."

* * * *

In the bookstore, Ayanna smiled at the customers she was helping and handed them their purchases. "Have a great day," she said as they walked away.

Her gaze moved back across the corridor to the flower shop where a handsome man talked to Lauren. His faded jeans seemed to mould themselves to his lower half. A beige shirt hugged his torso and defined his upper arms as it conformed to them. A whisper of familiarity skated across her skin, but she shook it off.

"Figures," she muttered to herself. "She's either getting a dinner date or he's buying flowers for his wife." Allowing herself one lingering look at the dark-haired man, she walked over to a box of new inventory waiting for her attention and got back to work.

As she finished putting the last book on the stand specifically for military reading, Lauren entering the bookstore with a silly grin on her face as she walked.

"Hey, Ayanna," she said in her typical, upbeat manner.

"Lauren," Ayanna responded with a grin. "I saw that handsome man hanging over your counter."

A blush moved up her friend's face. "Oh, that...that was Lieutenant Taylor."

"Ooohhhh," Ayanna teased. "And what are you doing with him later? Or should I say *to* him."

I knew a Taylor once, but that was a different lifetime ago.

"Shut up, you. He was returning my purse, well your purse. He was very impressed with its contents. The playbill, the poetry book..."

"Why would he be impressed with that?"

"I guess he doesn't meet many people who read American poets anymore."

Ayanna rolled her eyes. "And I suppose you told him the lead in *Phantom* was just *so* dreamy." The deepening flush on Lauren's face gave her the answer. Ayanna shook her head. She'd let Lauren borrow the purse for a date and was still waiting on the return of her items. Things she'd forgotten were in the purse at the time. "Shame on you for trying to pass off those things as yours."

"Well, I was just trying to make an impression."

Ayanna burst out laughing. She couldn't help it. "Can you even tell me one of the poets in that book?"

Collagen-injected lips pursed as Lauren thought.

With a friendly yet knowing smirk, Ayanna patted Lauren's arm as she moved to the counter and the customer who waited there.

Fifteen minutes later, Ayanna sat down outside the Exchange at the small table and took out her lunch. A few moments later, Lauren joined her and they chatted easily while they ate.

"Is Erma dropping off Devon today?"

Ayanna smiled. "Yes. Yes, she is."

Devon Lamar Barker was her three-year-old son. Back when all she'd cared about were parties, she'd gone to a Thunderbirds air show demonstration with a friend in Albuquerque while on a break from undergraduate school.

And had gotten pregnant.

There'd been a huge party. Lots to see. Lots to do. Well, only one for Ayanna. She'd met him at the beer tent. His name was Michael Kelly Taylor.

He was a handsome man. A few inches over six feet. Golden tan skin, all over. His hair was mocha brown and soft to touch. His dark, sensual, chocolaty gaze had felt like satin when it had touched her. He was beautifully constructed – a body that belonged in a sculptor's studio, chiselled from granite or marble. Yet, his touch had been warm and tender.

He'd told her he was staying in Albuquerque at Kirkland Air Force Base. She hadn't known what that meant exactly, but she'd gathered he was military. And assumed Air Force.

Honestly, she didn't care. It was a combination of things. The evening air, the buzz from alcohol, the fact she was wild and impulsive. All combined, it had left her with no desire to leave his presence. Topping it all had been how the mere touch of his callused fingers sent tremors through her body.

Michael had kept her cradled against his chest during the firework display that had rounded out the night's festivities, his body keeping the cool desert air at bay. The memory of that night was imprinted on her soul.

"Ayanna, are you listening to me?"

Blinking rapidly, Ayanna shook her head, dragged back to the moment. "Sorry Lauren, I got lost there for a sec."

"From the dreamy expression on your face, I'd bet it was a guy."

Ayanna blushed. "Yeah, it was."

"Who?" Lauren asked, more than ready to dish some dirt with her friend.

"Devon's father."

A blonde eyebrow rose. "You haven't ever talked much about him. I guess I always assumed your relationship had ended badly."

A short bark of laughter slipped out. "Relationship? Let's just say I was being 'liberated' and such. Went to the Thunderbirds air show and the fireworks afterward. The rest was history."

Lauren opened and shut her mouth. "Is Devon's father military?" Her head cocked to the side in question.

Ayanna shrugged. "He said he was staying at Kirkland. To be honest...I didn't care. I was at lot younger then, still trying to figure out what I wanted to do."

Lauren smirked. "Since I've met Devon, I'd say you *did* do something you wanted to."

Running a hand down her face, Ayanna narrowed her eyes. Leaning forward, she whispered in a conspiratorial tone, "I did and it was *wonderful*. I have never, and I mean never, felt like that."

"What happened between you two?" Lauren asked.

"What do you mean? We had a wonderful night and then...parted ways."

"I mean, why didn't you tell him about Devon?"

"I didn't know until I was two months pregnant." Ayanna smoothed out her sandwich bag and put it back into her lunch container. "I had to settle down and get my life in order — and fast — so that's what I did."

"Were you scared he wouldn't —"

"No," Ayanna interrupted. "I didn't even think about him at all. The second I got the news I was pregnant, my whole world shifted. It was all about the precious life I carried. And has been ever since. Having Devon is the greatest thing that could have happened to me. Sure, I wish circumstances had been different. Like marriage beforehand, but it didn't happen that way."

She placed her empty water bottle inside the container as well. "I wasn't anywhere near New Mexico and didn't have extra money to attempt to find him. Okay, perhaps I was scared of rejection." Ayanna fiddled with her lunch box. "Perhaps I was scared to hear anything negative out of his mouth. I wanted to remember him as he was when we spent the night together. Passionate. Sexual. Erotic. Not angry and accusing. I had enough on my plate to deal with."

Lauren smiled softly and reached her hand across the round wire table. "I'm glad we became friends. And I am going to stop questioning you about this, because —" She pointed to the left.

Ayanna followed her friend's finger with her gaze and smiled. Erma, her babysitter who was really more like a grandmother, and her son were heading towards them. Devon churned his little legs as fast as he could, a silly grin on his face.

Standing, she started to walk to him.

"*Ayanna*? Ayanna, is that you?"

Looking behind her, she met the gaze of the person who called out to her and froze. Staring back at her was the most sensual pair of dark chocolate eyes she'd seen in her life.

Michael Kelly Taylor.

Dear sweet Jesus. Am I imagining him? How come he still looks so damn good?

She allowed her gaze to roam over his body. Everything around her faded as his stare touched her like the lover he'd been to her that one wonderful night. Her lower body reacted much the same way it had the night they had met. Suddenly, she grew damp. Her hand touched the base of her throat. *All it takes is a look and I am ready. Ready for him to...* Mentally shaking the direction of those thoughts away, Ayanna fought to moisturise her dry throat. *How is it when my mouth goes dry my pussy is drenched?*

"Michael?" she murmured.

The afternoon sun glinted off his dark hair. Those muscles covering his body were more defined than they had been before. His body rippled with power and the promise of safety.

In slow motion, she took in his jeans and the shirt and realised he was the same man who'd returned her purse to Lauren. The same man who'd given her more pleasure than anyone had a right to experience.

He stepped closer. "Ayanna?"

Michael couldn't believe it. The last time he'd seen Ayanna, she'd been sound asleep in the king-sized bed of her room at the Marriott. Her naked body had contrasted beautifully with the light sheets that had covered her.

He'd sat beside her and stroked her hair. She'd murmured incoherently and snuggled further into the feather duvet, never waking. Trailing a finger along her jaw line, he'd whispered, "Goodbye, Ayanna," and left. Like any man would after a one-night stand.

He hadn't wanted to leave her but his leave was up and he'd needed to get back to work. Before they'd ended up in the bed, he'd asked her where she was from. She'd hedged with her answer.

That hadn't mattered. The second his hand had brushed the small of her back in the beer tent line, he'd been lost. The nutmeg tone of her skin had seemed to surround the lighter tan of his and cradle it. The jolt that rocketed through his body at that simple touch had amazed him.

He'd made love to her, and for the moment she had soothed the restlessness inside him. And now, she was before him in a different state and looking better than ever. *I haven't experienced anything remotely close since the night in her arms. I want that back.*

She'd changed her hair. Now springy curls moved with each motion she made. She wore dark blue jeans and a floral top that only fastened on one dark, creamy shoulder, leaving the other one bare. She was curvier than he remembered, and he longed to explore her new body. Wanted to bury his face in the side of her neck and relearn her scent all over again.

"Ayanna?" he asked again, noticing how her eyes kept flickering to the side. Following her line of sight, he spied an older woman walking with one of the cutest little boys he had ever seen.

The child wore a tank top with a picture of a basketball on it. The shorts he wore matched the colours of the top. His head was shaved almost bald, but there were telltale signs of growth. However, it was the sparkle in his dark eyes and a smile that stood out against his brown skin that brought a grin to Michael's face.

The fierce concentration on the young man's face was apparent, but so was the joy he had as he walked in the afternoon sun towards his goal. One small hand reached out and his fingers wiggled with anticipation. From his lips poured the word "Mama" over and over again.

Michael experienced a serious pang of envy when Ayanna turned and opened her arms to the overjoyed child. Of course, such an adorable child would have a stunning mother. She went down on one knee and embraced the little boy. As her arms wrapped around his body, she stood back up. She glanced at Michael over her shoulder before returning her complete attention to the woman who'd walked with the child.

Glancing down at the table where Ayanna had been sitting, he noticed the clerk from the floral shop. He moved towards her and stood near the chair Ayanna had left. Lauren's eyes focused on him.

"Do you know her well?" Michael asked without looking at her, opting instead to watch Ayanna.

"Yes, Lieutenant, I do." Lauren stood, as well, and watched him as if she'd just figured out a huge secret.

"Is she married? Is that her child?" The questions rattled from him as quickly as if fired from a semi-automatic gun. Logically, he knew it was her child, but part of him refused to accept it.

He didn't wait for an answer. Three long strides placed him beside Ayanna.

It was sweltering out and yet this woman smelled fresh. He recognised the smell of her soap. It was light and gentle, soothing like baby powder.

She stiffened and he knew she'd sensed him. His eyes moved to the hand splayed on the boy's back. No wedding ring.

She's not wearing a ring, his mind crowed.
This woman was his destiny.
"Hello, Ayanna."

Chapter Two

Ayanna didn't know what to do. When her eyes settled on the man who'd fathered her child, she froze. How did one go from saying "Hello" to "Oh by the way I want you to meet *our* son?"

Her fingers instinctively tightened on Devon's jersey. Michael's light woodsy scent flooded her senses. If she hadn't been holding her child...*their* child...her legs might have given out.

Devon struggled to be set down, so while she assisted him in that, she answered, "Hello again, Michael." *Please go away before I lose control of my emotions.*

He didn't grant her wish. Instead, he knelt beside her and smiled at the child who was thrilled to be on the ground. "And who is this handsome little man?"

"Hi," the child chortled. Then as his brown eyed gaze landed on Lauren, he let out a squeal of "Lr'en" and ran to her, demanding she pick him up.

Ayanna began to stand as she felt his hand on hers. Glancing over at him, she asked the first thing that popped into her mind, "What are you doing here?"

Michael's eyes sparkled. "I'm stationed here. What about you?"

"I'm...I...I'm...I...work here and now, I've got to get my son home." She pulled her hand from his intoxicating touch and stood. Stepping away, she moved to Erma who still stood silently and kissed her goodbye. "Thanks, Erma. We'll see you tomorrow."

The old lady nodded and walked off after kissing Devon goodbye.

"Ayanna?" Michael asked as she sent him another nervous look.

"It was good to see you," she managed to stutter. "Goodbye, Michael."

"Da-da!" Devon's voice rang loud and clear like the bells of Notre Dame. Both Ayanna and Michael looked at him. He was pointing in Michael's direction.

A blush burned up her cheeks. Beside her, Michael laughed, allowing her to relax. "Introduce me to your son, Ayanna." His command was soft, but she heard him easily.

Together, they walked to where Lauren still stood with Devon. He reached out his arms the second they got within range, but when Ayanna reached out for him, he stuck out his bottom lip and reached towards Michael instead.

Michael's mouth quirked and Ayanna knew full well it was because of the exasperated expression on her face. Taking Devon, she said, "We'll see you later, Lauren."

Lauren smiled and kissed Devon who still happily repeated "Da-da" and grabbed in Michael's direction. "Bye," she said, then went back inside to return to work.

"Down, Mama. Down!" Devon demanded.

Ayanna complied. Once he was down, Devon spread his arms wide and began imitating the jets that roared above them. She glanced at Michael as he stared at her son.

"His name is Devon," she said.

Michael's sensuous gaze met hers. Ayanna knew that look, the sleepy look that belied the sharpness of his observation skills. It was a look she'd received, right before he'd proved he'd been watching each of her reactions to his touch.

This time, his eyes turned shrewd.

"How old is he?" Michael asked as one strong arm shot out and kept the tottering child from falling over his feet. He smiled as Devon's hands closed over his forearm. "He looks about..." Michael trailed off and looked back up.

Ayanna shivered as comprehension dawned in his eyes. Squaring her shoulders, she met his gaze directly. "I have to get going. This is our afternoon to go to the park." She shouldered her son's bag. "Devon, let's go."

"Wait a minute," Michael said as her hand closed around her son's smaller one. He stood in a smooth motion. "Is this...is he...am I...?"

Tightening her hold on Devon's soft hand, she swallowed. *I had no idea it would be this hard to admit I kept his child from him.* Granted he *had* been the one to leave first, but by the same token she hadn't wanted to share information with him. Why? Because it was a one-night stand. This just happened to be one with consequences.

"Ayanna?" Michael placed a hand around her wrist.

"Lieutenant Taylor, how wonderful to see you," a thin brunette woman interrupted. She smiled as she stopped beside them. Her green eyes moved to where he held onto Ayanna then back up to his face. "Bridget was saying how excited she is that you're stopping by for dinner."

Michael surprised Ayanna by not releasing her hand. Instead, he intertwined their fingers. "I'm sorry, Ma'am, but I told her I couldn't make dinner this week."

The woman's eyes narrowed and she looked back at Ayanna before nodding. "Well, I guess my husband will be disappointed as well, then."

Michael sent her a tight-lipped smile. "He's already been made well aware of the change in plans, Ma'am."

"Well, apparently Bridget hasn't. But since she's coming right now, you can explain it all to her."

Ayanna swallowed back her hurt. *Why should I expect him to be single?* Gently, she unhooked their hands and smiled at him. "I've got to get my son to the park. Um…" She dug around in her pocket and pulled out a piece of paper, writing on it. "…here."

Michael took it and looked at the address before putting it into his front pocket. "I'll talk to you later then, Ayanna. It was wonderful to see you again."

"Yes it was, Michael." She picked up her child, needing his closeness. Her eyes landed on the pretty woman approaching them. Stepping away from the man who had the ability to make her forget everything, she looked back at him, her eyes solemn.

He met her eyes and cocked his head.

"He is," she murmured so only the two of them could hear. Then she walked off, not wanting to witness another woman taking his attentions.

Michael's gaze followed her as she carried Devon through the parking lot. His eyes stayed on her retreating form until she disappeared from view.

I have a child? I have a child! Michael couldn't let Ayanna leave like this. He took two steps then froze as Bridget placed a hand on his arm. As the commander's daughter began chatting, Michael knew he'd lost Ayanna for the moment.

He wanted to get this straightened out and then he wanted to make love to her. Over and over again.

Michael made his excuses as soon as he could and drove to the address on the paper she'd given him. It wasn't much to look at; the whole building needed work. He went home and waited until six when he hoped she'd be home from the park.

Ayanna? His mind repeated her name over and over as he got out of his car and headed up the dark stairs to the number she'd written on the paper. He knocked on the water-stained door.

"Who is it?" Ayanna's voice reached him.

"Michael."

He heard locks disengage before the door swung open. The light from behind her highlighted the dark auburn tint to her hair. Beautiful.

"You came."

"You honestly didn't think I wouldn't come, did you? You have my son." There was no menace in his voice, just fact. He looked over her head and smiled as he saw Devon playing with blocks on the living room floor.

"Come on in," she said. He walked past her and straight to where Devon was and knelt beside him. Michael heard the locks engaged but didn't turn around. The big brown eyes that looked up at him struck him speechless.

Devon showed him a block and smiled. "Hi," he said before turning his attention back to his toys.

"Hello, Devon." Michael reached for a block and turned it over in his lean fingers.

"Peez."

Michael looked away from the block and saw Devon holding out his hand for it.

"Peez."

"Oh, sorry." He handed it back with a smile. The child babbled a toddler's version of thank you while Michael looked over to the kitchen table with one chair and a highchair at it and saw Ayanna watching their private interaction with a nervous expression on her beautiful face.

Pushing up from the floor, he walked over to her. "I think we should talk." His gaze took in the books on the shaky table—all of them about Pharmacology.

"You're right."

* * * *

"No. I don't think that would be a good idea." Ayanna shook her head. Michael's suggestion didn't feel right to her.

He blew out an exasperated breath. They'd been going over this for the past two hours. A while ago, Devon had been put to bed then they'd continued arguing over the same thing. He didn't like her and his son living here.

"What isn't a good idea? You need to get out of this place. I have room at my apartment. I can watch him when you're in school or need to study. Let me help you."

"I just…" She let the words hang in the air.

He shifted his weight on the couch and watched her, she'd opted to reclaim her seat at the kitchen table. "Look, I have a three bedroom townhouse. Devon can have his own room." He licked his lips. "And so can you. Please, Ayanna. Let me help with *our* son."

"Why aren't you more upset that I didn't tell you?" she questioned, truly baffled. She didn't understand why he wasn't yelling at her.

"Would that make you feel better? Do you want me to yell at you? I *am* furious that you didn't tell me, but what good will yelling do for either of us? I want to be a part of my son's life and not just by giving you money."

Ayanna ran her hands over her face. "I...I just don't want you to be—"

His jaw clenched. "Don't you *dare* say inconvenienced. I could never be inconvenienced by my own son."

His son. Not her. Her heart sank before she could stop it. "Okay, we'll give it a trial run. But I'm putting my stuff in storage in case it doesn't work out."

Michael grinned. Standing, he moved to her side and tipped her head up. "We'll get you moved in tomorrow. I'll be here around seven. Does that work for you?"

Ayanna couldn't answer him. All it took was his touch and she was a bumbling mess of nerves. When a knowing grin touched the corners of his mouth, she found her words. "Okay, we'll be ready. I just hope you know what you're getting into."

One hand caressed her cheek. "I know exactly what I'm doing. Now, I should get going and clean up my office so it's is ready for Devon." His head lowered so their lips were scant millimetres apart. "Goodnight, Ayanna." He settled his lips along hers and gave her one of the most tender kisses of her life.

Her body shivered with longing. And she didn't quite catch the whimper that escaped as he backed away. The flare in his eyes told her that he heard it. *Jesus, I would walk through the fires of hell to experience this man's touch again.*

Michael traced her lower lip with his thumb before kissing her again. Then he grabbed his keys and walked to the door, saying over his shoulder. "Tomorrow, Ayanna. Lock this behind me."

She stayed motionless in her chair as he walked out the door and disappeared from view. After it closed, she got up to lock it again. She looked around her tiny place.

"This is a good move. More space for Devon. His father in his life." Trying to assure herself and keep the doubt at bay, she began to pack her few belongings in boxes and suitcases. She took only the bare necessities for herself, making sure that Devon came first. All his toys and clothes were most important. She also called Erma and filled her in on the change in plans so the woman didn't show up the next day.

It was after midnight before Ayanna climbed into bed, her meagre items packed and ready. She'd clean tomorrow after the place was empty. The lingering taste of Michael's kiss still on her lips, she murmured his name as she lay on her twin size bed and pulled the sheets over her.

* * * *

Michael was at her door a few moments before seven. He knocked and couldn't explain his relief when she opened the door, a shy smile on her face.

Today she wore a pair of dark green warm-up pants and a grey T-shirt. Her hair called out for him to touch it, to sink his fingers into the curls and kiss her until neither of them knew their own names.

His gaze dropped to her lips, which were free of gloss and he groaned as the memory of her taste floated to the surface of his mind. "Morning, Ayanna," he whispered.

"Come on in," she said. "We're ready. I just have to clean after its empty."

He picked up on the nervousness in her tone. "This will work out, Ayanna. Trust me." His hand travelled over the

39

small of her back as he moved to where Devon ran in circles with his toy plane. The engine noises he made were in sync with his "flight path."

"Good morning, Devon," Michael said as he crouched down beside the pattern the child was wearing into the already-worn rug.

Those big brown eyes, darker than his mother's looked right back at him. In fact, they looked like the dark chocolate colour of his own eyes. "Hi," Devon spoke. One hand shoved the grey plane at Michael. "P'ane," he announced proudly.

A knock on the door, interrupted before Michael said anything. He moved to stand behind Ayanna as she opened it and admitted a group of his friends who said hello to Michael.

"Okay, Ayanna," he said as he lifted Devon into his arms, "tell them what you want put in storage and what you want to keep with you."

Obviously unnerved at the looks the men were sending her and Michael, Ayanna cleared her throat first. Then she began pointing to items that were going. The men left and with Devon playing with a toy, Ayanna and Michael made short work out of the cleaning.

* * * *

Ayanna followed Michael in her vehicle, Devon secure in his car seat in the back. Unbidden her mind drifted to the man she was moving in with. Michael's powerfully fit body appeared in her head. Lowering over her, his hard cock slipping between the lips of her wet pussy. The way his sensual eyes grew lustful as he drove into her. Over and over again.

Ayanna shifted on her vinyl seat as her belly clenched with longing. Squirming helplessly, she swallowed and thought a bit more. How was she going to be able to control her rampaging lust when it came to this man?

Memories swarmed her. The water droplets cascading down his naked physique in the shower. The dimple in his right butt cheek. The feel of his cock in her hands, mouth, and how he tasted as his cum shot down her throat.

She whimpered as her body reacted to the images as if they were happening.

"Get a grip, Barker," she admonished herself and did her best to focus on something other than the tall, muscular, smouldering-eyed Michael Taylor.

It didn't work.

As Michael pulled into an apartment complex, she followed and parked beside him. Her gaze took in the nice two-story buildings. It looked nothing like where she'd lived previously.

The lawns were well manicured. The buildings were not in need of painting. In fact, all of it was amazing. The kind of place she wanted to be — a place where she'd be safe going out at night, a place where she'd be okay letting Devon play in the front yard.

"Mama!" Devon yelled from the backseat as he began kicking his legs.

"I'm coming." She unbuckled her belt and found Michael had opened her door. His hand lingered longer than necessary against her skin as he helped her out.

"I'll get him." Michael moved back to the door. With ease he lifted the three and a half year old from his seat. "Let's go, little man."

After he shut the door he glanced again at Ayanna and said, "We'll get you two inside and then I will come back for the rest of your things. The truck is here and your stuff is being put in your new rooms. My townhouse is the one at the end."

Grabbing two bags for Devon from the trunk, Ayanna followed Michael. She felt as if every eye in the development was on her. Watching her, judging her. Considering it was early morning on Sunday, however, there weren't people outside, so she knew it was her imagination.

Her stomach knotted up as Michael unlocked the door to his townhouse. She followed him across the tiled foyer and into the open and airy downstairs. The carpeted parts were done in a slate grey and all the furniture was beige leather. She didn't see any personal touches around the place. It was much larger than hers — and this was just the downstairs.

Walking behind him to the stairs, she automatically identified things that needed to be done to child-proof his place. She bit back a worried snort as she saw his large television.

When they got to the top of the stairs, Michael pointed to the left. "That's my room. Devon's is in the middle and your room is down there. I gave Devon the smallest room and yours is in the back so you can have some privacy." The men who'd moved the items smiled at her as they passed them. They nodded at Michael.

"Sounds great. But we really need to go over rent and stuff like…" She stopped as his eyes speared her. "What?"

Michael opened the door to Devon's room and set the child down on the floor among the toys that were there. His furniture was already set up. Everything was more than she could have hoped for.

She blinked as Michael's attention turned from Devon to her. He stalked her until her back was against the corner of the doorjamb. Her eyes widened as inch by inch her personal space was eviscerated.

"I am not charging you rent. You're the mother of my child. First thing tomorrow, we're going to get both of you on my medical plan and get you a dependant's card."

A dependant's card? "I'm not marrying you."

"Yes, you are. I won't force my attentions on you, but you *will* marry me and you *will* take the health insurance I can offer. It will help you with the cost of your schooling, too."

She shook her head furiously until one of his hands gripped her chin and held it immobile. His mouth covered hers and his tongue swept inside.

Ayanna clasped his sleeves as their bodies pressed closer. Just as it had been the first night they'd touched, each response was explosive and set her body on fire. Her craving for him flared almost out of control. She wanted to crawl all over his body and let his touch carry her away to the stars.

"We *are* getting married," he promised her as his mouth left hers.

"I agreed to move in—not marry you." Ayanna tried to step back but his hand swept behind her and kept her body pressed to his. His erection pressed into her.

"Ayanna," he said with increasing exasperation. "I'm willing to overlook the fact you kept my son from me. But this is the only way I know to give you protection and you *will* take it."

"What about your social life?" She couldn't bring herself to let go of his arms.

He smiled with more tenderness than anything else. "It doesn't matter. You and Devon matter." His lips brushed against hers again before he stepped away. "You stay here. I'll get the rest of your things and say goodbye to the guys."

His callused hand caressed the side of her face one more time before he moved past her to go back downstairs.

* * * *

Michael knew he was moving fast, but for the life of him, he didn't care. Part of him had fallen in love with Ayanna that night in New Mexico, and he'd hoped she'd come looking for him. He'd been disappointed when she hadn't.

Ayanna Genat Barker had sent him into a tailspin he didn't think he'd ever want to escape. His body come alive again as if shooting through the sky in his F/A-18 or doing a series of night traps out on a carrier. That same rush he got from his job, he got from seeing a smile on Ayanna's face.

He smiled as he walked back to his house carrying Ayanna's bags. A family would make this place a home. The thought of making love to Ayanna in every room, on every piece of leather furniture, turned his gentle smile to a predatory one. The vision of her dark skinned body draped across his lighter furniture made his cock leap to attention. He adjusted his pants and continued towards his house.

Pushing open the front door, he momentarily froze at the familiar sight of his bland decorating scheme. As the musical strands of childish laughter floated down the stairs, he relaxed and shut the door with his foot then headed up to the second floor.

He stopped in the doorway of his old office, now Devon's room and watched Ayanna reading to his son. She sat on the floor, her voice full of expression as she told the story, but the words were meaningless to Michael. All his focus was on her mouth. He couldn't move past the way her lips pursed to form the words. So plump, so luscious, so damn tempting.

44

In a flash, he saw her sucking his cock, her gorgeous mouth wrapped around him. Her tongue would run around the head, pulling him further into her web of passion.

He bit back a groan as his penis jerked adamantly. Squeezing his eyes shut, he shook as more pictures exploded before his mind's eye. Ayanna sprawled across his bed, wet and waiting for him. Her firm body as she rode him, cradling him with her heat. Her full breasts swaying before him, luring him to taste and suckle them.

Forcing down the unrelenting yearning to possess this woman, he cleared his throat.

She smiled warily when she looked up.

"I have to go out and pick up some things," she said, setting aside the book and standing. "But we'll be back later."

His gut clenched. The idea of losing her again raced through him. Fear slithered through him. What if she disappeared with Devon? What if he lost her before he'd really even had her? What if?

"What do you need?" he asked, his voice sharp with suspicion.

"I have to childproof your house or Devon will be into everything."

Child-proofing. I didn't even think of that. "Okay, let's go." His fear vanished, replaced by shame. *I should have trusted her.*

"I can do this without you."

"Ayanna," Michael growled. "Don't make this a battle. We need to get another car seat anyway, for my vehicle, so we may as well take it and that way we will have more room with whatever you need to get. Besides…if you keep insisting on arguing with me, I'm gonna insist on making up." His body tensed even if his voice didn't reflect it. Ayanna understood.

"Fine," she agreed immediately. "Let's get going."

Chapter Three

Michael opened the door and entered his home. His dark brown eyes took in the scattered toys around the living room, the gate at the bottom of the stairs, the child's beanbag chair and a blow up chair beside a Big Wheel. It had been a month since he'd moved in Ayanna and Devon. His place was totally different, and he loved it. He had a family, even if she didn't want to tell anyone about the marriage and insisted on sleeping in a separate room.

That was his next hurdle.

His nose was filled by the smell of food cooking even as he caught sight of Ayanna cleaning up the living room. She wore a purple shirt and a floral skirt, which was knotted up mid-thigh, allowing him to see her beautiful legs as she moved.

He knew she thought she was fat but he loved her curves. She was a gorgeous woman. Having his child had only enhanced her beauty. He grinned as she muttered to herself while she cleaned.

"Hey, Ayanna." A groan slipped from deep in his throat as she turned towards him and she licked those full, tempting, succulent lips of hers.

"How was work?" she asked as she closed the lid of Devon's toy chest.

"Wonderful. There isn't much that compares to being a pilot." His eyes moved with definite purpose over her body. "There are some things though."

"Right," she snorted. "Dinner should be ready in a bit."

He dropped his bag by the door and walked further into the room. "Where's Devon?"

"Still napping. We went swimming today, and he's really exhausted. I'm letting him sleep until food's ready."

"Be right back," Michael said. He took the stairs two at a time and headed to his room to change.

Ayanna sank onto the couch as he went. It was getting more and more difficult to ignore the attraction between them. Especially when Michael looked so damn good walking through the door in his flight suit. Damn, it made him look good. Everything he wore made him look good, but that suit…just…aroused her. She sighed. Not even in the same room with him for three minutes and she had wet panties. *I should give up wearing them, yeesh.*

Standing, she went into the kitchen and checked on dinner — spaghetti and meatballs.

"Damn you, Michael," she cursed as she ran a hand over her skirt before dipping a spoon into the sauce for a taste. "Why do you make me want you?"

"Is wanting me really all that horrible?" a deep voice asked from behind her.

She screamed and jumped, dropping the spoon. The hot sauce splashed onto her hand. *Of course he would hear that.*

"Damn, I'm sorry. I didn't want to scare you. Give me your hand," he ordered, even as he took it himself and put it under cold water. "I'm sorry, baby. Does that feel better?"

Feel better? Sweet Jesus, I am about to jump you right here and now if you don't let go. Pulling her hand away, she shook off the water. "Fine, it's fine."

Michael reached around her and turned off the faucet. Grabbing her hand, he pressed his lips to the red mark on her smooth skin. "I'm so sorry. I didn't mean to startle you."

You have got to stop touching me, man. "I'm fine. Thanks." She pulled her hand back.

"Ayanna," he murmured as his fingers delved into the curls on her head.

Give me the strength to keep him away.

Her palms rose between them. His smouldering eyes tugged at every fibre of her being, crying for her to give in.

Instead of backing off, he stepped closer so her hands rested against the hard planes of his chest. He caressed her skull as the distance between them was diminished.

"We can't..." she forced out even as she traced the contours of his chiselled torso.

"We can," he whispered back. "Ayanna, we can." One leg pushed between hers, pressing his full-fledged erection into her belly.

"No. We shouldn't." Her senses were swimming.

He lowered his head so their mouths almost touched. "Ayanna," he groaned. His tongue traced her lower lip before he sucked it into his mouth.

Her body clenched with need. She arched her back and moved her hands up his chest to lace them behind his neck.

"Yes," she mumbled back as his kiss dominated her very being.

He put both of his hands on her face as he made love to her mouth. His body pressed hers to the sink as the intensity of the kiss increased one hundred fold. Their hips instinctively mimed the action they craved to share.

His hands moved down her shoulders and along the contours of her body. When he touched the bare skin of her waist she whimpered into his mouth. Her eyes flew open then closed as waves of pleasure erupted in her.

"Ayanna. You fit so perfectly in my arms."

"Michael." She pulled him closer so they seemed to meld together. He lifted her to sit on the edge of the sink and she wrapped her legs around his lean waist. His mouth nibbled down her neck, following the V in her shirt. His rough tongue swept over the exposed tops of her breasts. She dropped her head back to allow him easier access. One hand rested on the cool countertop while her other remained pressed against the back of his head. Her body shivered with her desire to have his length burrowed deep inside her again. Unconsciously, her legs tightened around him.

Michael inched up her shirt even as his tongue continued to relearn the subtle taste of her skin. Her breasts were sensitive and she wanted him to suckle on them.

"Please," she moaned.

"Look at your breasts. They're fuller than before. Damn, you're beautiful." Michael sucked one breast in his mouth, shirt and all, while his hands covered her belly. He took one hand and teased the soft skin of her inner thigh. She trembled as his touch inflamed her. Working feverishly to get some moisture back in her mouth, she mewled with pleasure.

"Ayanna," he mumbled, releasing her breast with a pop. His free hand shoved up her top and seconds later his mouth latched onto her other breast. Bra and all.

He slid one thick finger under the edge of her underwear and ran it up between her pussy lips. Her juices dripped out of her. She pressed his head tighter against her. His finger circled her swollen clit before thrusting inside her.

"Oh yeah!" she hissed as her hips gyrated down on his digit. He added another. And another. "Oh shit!" she rasped.

Her body burned and she writhed shamelessly, coming hard on his plunging fingers. Her screams grew louder and louder as the palm of his hand ground against her overly sensitive clit.

His mouth left her breast and he nibbled her neck near her ear. "I want my cock buried balls deep in your hot pussy."

His blatant admission combined with the exquisite torture he delivered sent another orgasm crashing through her. Her body contracted around his fingers as her hips rose off the countertop, the evidence of her pleasure running down his hand.

"Michael!" Her scream couldn't be contained.

"Right here." He kissed her. He kept his fingers moving as she gradually came back down from the rapture his touch had elevated her to. Still his touch placed her back on the edge within moments.

He rotated his thumb over her swollen nub as his fingers continued to plunge deep inside her, her thick cream covering them. Her body shuddered as his expert caress sent her over the edge again.

"Michael," she moaned as she bit her lower lip. She was drained, her throat dry and scratchy from her response to him. *I have no idea how many times this man just made me orgasm, I can't think straight.*

"This is what it should be like, Ayanna. Why do you continue to deny us pleasure?"

Reality washed over her, and she shoved him away.

She jumped from the counter and headed for the door, only to be jerked back against Michael's chest.

"You can't keep running." He pressed her hand over his swollen erection. "This…this is what being around you does to me. I can smell your arousal. We belong together." He put his coated fingers in his mouth and licked them clean. "You still taste like heaven." He groaned even as he released her. "Soon, Ayanna. Very soon."

She bolted from the kitchen, her heart pounding like she'd just completed a marathon. *I can't believe I let that happen.* Her body still felt electrified from the encounter as she ran upstairs. *I was like a goddamn pole dancer and used his hand as the pole.*

In her room, she slumped against the cool wall and tried to sort out her feelings. How long could she truly fight her desire for this man? Sure, she was married to him, but he'd only done it for his son. "What am I doing? I can't get involved with him. *Can I?*" She shook her head violently. "No. No. No! I can't."

Why not, her mind taunted.

"This is just a business arrangement." The throbbing between her legs told her she was wrong. *Then he wouldn't have insisted on getting married. He could have just put Devon on his health plan.*

"Fucking conscience," she swore. "I don't want to be involved with him. It's better to protect myself now before he finds the woman he really wants to be with. It won't hurt as much that way."

What was the interaction in the kitchen if he didn't want you?

"I better figure it out." The wet panties she wore had her adding, "And fast." As she changed, she began a mantra of 'business relationship.'

She was no fool. She'd sensed him watching her at night, while she put Devon down for bed. His eyes would grow all soft and tender until he met her gaze, then his killer eyes would turn possessive and damn near primal. Flames would lick her skin where his eyes touched her.

Everyday he'd found more and more reasons to linger with each caress he gave her, be it when he took Devon from her, offered to help her clean, or just walked past her. He seemed to be shirtless a lot more, as well. And as soon as Devon went down for the night, Michael would invariably show up at her door to say goodnight.

Every night, his wishes for a wonderful night's sleep were echoed by contact. A touch which grew longer, more personal, and more heated every time it occurred. It had started as a stroke on the back of her hand, now he ran his fingers down the side of her face and along the back of her neck, before leaning in close and whispering in her ear. "Have a wonderful night, my wife. My beautiful Ayanna."

If she was awake when he left for work, he'd make sure to say something similar and leave her longing for more. For the life of her, she wanted to give in and see what it would be like to have a true relationship with him.

Pasting a smile on her face, a calmer Ayanna opened her door and headed downstairs to finish their meal. Five minutes later, Michael strolled in with Devon who'd just woken. This time her smile was unforced.

"Mama!" Devon said as he stomped across the floor and latched onto her leg.

"Hey, baby." One hand tenderly brushed the top of his head before she returned her attention to putting the final few items on the table. Even so, her eyes kept drifting back to Michael. His eyes were on her and they still blazed with unquenched thirst and a promise. A promise to finish what they'd started.

Michael watched as she moved. Instinctively she seemed to know where Devon was and always managed to step around him. As they sat down for dinner, Devon played with his spaghetti, eating it one piece at a time.

"Are you still free this afternoon or did you need to get more studying done?" Michael asked. His voice showed none of the ardour he felt for her. He realised he had to be careful on how he proceeded from here.

Taking a drink of water, she answered. "I can handle watching him if you have plans. Don't worry about it. I've studied with him around before."

"No, that's not it at all." He grabbed Devon's cup before it toppled. "I wanted to take both of you to the base and show him the planes."

"P'ane, p'ane, p'ane!" Devon chortled.

"Eat first, sport," Michael said, keeping his gaze on Ayanna. "What do you think?"

She smiled and it warmed him to the core. "Sure. I'm game."

She got up to take care of the dishes.

Michael frowned. "Just put them in the dishwasher and we can go." *Although just watching you walk around is tempting.*

"I am so used to doing them by hand."

He walked to her and kissed the back of her neck as Devon ran to the living room. "I know. But you don't need to do them that way anymore." Spinning her in his arms, he continued to kiss her.

Ayanna struggled against him for about two seconds before she sighed into his mouth and gave over to the power of his kiss.

He tucked her in closer to his chest. "Let's go."

"I'll be changed in a flash." She pulled back.

Michael followed, eliminating the distance again. "Need some help?" he purred. He watched her eyes flutter.

"N…n…no."

"Are you sure?" He slid on hand up her skirt at the knot high on her thigh. Her eyes glossed over with passion.

"I'm sure," she panted as his finger slid closer to the juncture of her thighs.

He looked over her shoulder before glancing back at her. His hand moved over the front of her panties. "You're wet for me." His cock pressed insistently against his jeans.

"I should get changed." Her words were barely audible.

"I want to taste you, Ayanna." He leaned in close to her ear. "Tell me I can." Light, feathery strokes moved across the increasingly damp underwear. Her mouth moved and he only just heard her faint 'yes.'

Michael groaned as he delved his index finger inside her. His hard erection throbbed as he withdrew his finger and sucked it clean.

"I need you," he said. His timbre was lower than usual as he let her out of his arms. He watched her leave and swore under his breath as he attempted to find a more comfortable position for his engorged cock.

* * * *

The guard at the gate snapped out a salute as they passed and entered the base. Turning into the parking lot, Michael found a spot and parked the SUV. Quickly, he got out. Ayanna was slower to follow.

"Coming, sweetheart?" he asked from the back door where he was pulling out Devon.

Smiling at him, she nodded and climbed out. Immediately, she felt nervous. She was swamped with that belief that everyone was watching her and judging her. It was her own personal demon, the belief that everyone wanted to pass judgment on her. Maybe it would be different with Michael beside her. She looked for him. He waited on the other side of his vehicle.

"Let's go," she said with more bravado than she felt.

Devon between them, they walked towards the jets lining the main road into Naval Air Station Oceana. Michael glanced at her. "Everything okay?"

"Yes, I just haven't been here aside from…" She trailed off.

"When we got married?" he asked.

"Yes," she muttered.

Michael shook his head. Ayanna was so strong and passionate about some things, but when it came to their relationship, she was still unsure. It was all crystal clear to him. They were a family. He'd happily stay with her for the rest of their lives. He wanted to have another child and be there for the birth. He wanted to see their children grow, get married, and have children of their own.

He'd recognised it the second he had seen her again. That restlessness inside him had vanished like it had the first time they met. Two halves of the same whole.

You are my life, Ayanna.

By now Devon had seen the jets and tried to hurry along the adults. Michael laughed and swung him up on his shoulders and hurried towards the object of his son's affection.

Ayanna followed at a slower pace and allowed her eyes to roam over the way Michael's jeans fit him and how his blue shirt pulled taut across his shoulders. Her mouth watered at the way his rippling muscles easily flexed to support Devon and keep him safe from any harm. *Jesus, this man has me acting like a damn sex addict. I am in a constant state of arousal around him.* She swallowed the groan that threatened to slip out as her mind stripped away his clothes.

A few other people milled around the planes, talking and pointing at them while they read the information beside each one. She moved up beside a grey jet in time to overhear Michael say to Devon, "This is almost like what Daddy flies."

Patiently, he pointed out things to their son, his tone gentle. His eyes met hers and his nose crinkled as he grinned. Her physical response had her forcing down another shudder.

As she walked up to them, Michael leaned over and kissed her cheek, apparently not concerned with keeping their relationship a secret.

"You fly this?" Ayanna asked.

"Well, no. I fly the F/A-18E Super Hornet." Michael caressed the side of the grey plane, his passion for flying lighting his eyes.

"Boo," Devon announced as he pointed at the Blue Angel jet.

"That's right, it is blue," Michael said as he walked his son to the blue and yellow jet. "This is an F/A-18 Hornet."

"This isn't what they were flying in New Mexico, was it? For the Thunderbirds?" Ayanna asked as she hesitatingly touched the jet. Her body flushed as she remembered what had happened after the show.

"No," Michael answered. "The Air Force flies F-16's for the Thunderbirds." The gleam in his eyes told her he was remembering, as well.

"And what, if any, are they also called?" Ayanna wanted to keep that glow about him as he talked about planes. *He looks so hot with that fire in his eyes.* Her mind painted another erotic picture for her. She moaned softly.

"Fighting Falcon," he replied, smiling.

"Oh, I see." Ayanna pulled back her hand and wiped it on her thigh. She swallowed a few times, trying to find a way to understand the emotions moving through her. It scared her to know that he was up in the sky, flying one of these aircraft.

It was dangerous flying.

Okay, time for you to face it. You have feelings for him, and they're more than just sexual ones, her brain announced. Ayanna realised it was true, all of it. No matter how hard she tried to ignore it, there was a true connection between her and Michael. She could imagine them together when they were both old and grey. And it scared the hell out of her.

Before actually hearing him say he flew a fighter plane, it had been easy, to an extent, to ignore the flight suit and pretend his job was safe. The possibility of losing him to a woman was a way to keep him at arm's length. The thought that he might go to work and never come home...scared her shitless.

Her heart rate tripled when he sent her a private smile. The kind that made her believe he viewed her as the most beautiful woman in the world. *There goes my idea of maintaining a business-like relationship.* He licked his lips as his eyes roved over her. *It's like he reads my mind.*

Michael winked.

Ayanna trembled.

"Michael!"

She looked in the direction of the voice. A man on the other side of the street waved at Michael. Slanting a look at her husband, she saw him smile and wave back.

A few moments later, the blond-haired man reached them. He was a bit shorter than Michael but in the same excellent shape. "What's up, Taz?" he said. "Didn't think you would be here on your day off."

"What's up, Racer?" Michael shook the blond's hand.

"Just coming to see if I can get—" Racer snapped his mouth shut, suddenly noticing the child in Michael's arms. "Who's this cute little man?"

Michael slid an arm around Ayanna. "I want you to meet my wife, Ayanna, and our son, Devon. We're spending the afternoon looking at the planes."

Devon grinned and pointed at the Blue Angel replica aircraft. "P'ane," he proudly said.

If Racer was shocked, he didn't let it show. A wide grin appeared as he reached for Ayanna's hand. "Wow, what's a beauty like you doing with this one?" He bowed over the back of her hand. "It's a pleasure to meet you, Ayanna. I'm Lieutenant Pete Kysenzki, better known as Racer."

She smiled shyly. "Thank you. It's wonderful to meet you, as well."

Michael frowned at his friend. "Let go of my wife's hand, Racer."

Racer winked at her, then he looked at Devon. "Good thing he takes after his mom, instead of you, Taz."

"I know," Michael agreed. "He's a great looking child."

The blond man smiled. "I have to go. I have a date. I'll see you later on, and Mrs. Taylor, it was lovely to finally meet you." He waved one more time and took off in the direction from which he had arrived.

Ayanna looked at her husband who was watching her instead of his friend. "What did he mean by that Michael?"

"Just that he's been waiting to meet you. That's my RIO. My closest friend here. Of course, he knows I'm married." He kissed her again then walked to an older version of a Navy plane showing it to Devon.

"Your RIO? What the heck is a RIO?" Ayanna was totally lost.

"Radio Intercept Officer. He and I fly in the same plane."

Ayanna closed her mouth. She had plenty of questions but she had other things to mull over. Like how matter-of-factly he'd said that of course he'd told Pete he was married. *Another point in your favour Michael Taylor.*

If she was honest, she'd been concerned people wouldn't like her because she was black. She'd already been a stereotype, the single black woman who had a kid. *What if being with me hurts his career?* She swallowed. *Michael doesn't seem to care or he wouldn't have introduced you or married you.* Running a hand over her face, Ayanna walked closer and watched her family. Eventually, Michael's deep voice soothed her frayed nerves. His actions with Devon were another huge point in his favour.

* * * *

On the way home from the base, Michael had picked up kerbside service from a local restaurant. At the moment, he was alone in the kitchen. As he finished wiping down the counters, he grinned as he recalled his earlier encounter on them with his wife.

He growled low in his throat at the recollection of how her tight, wet channel gripped his fingers. And how she tasted... Oh God. Even now, the memory of the look of her flushed skin as she cried her pleasure to the room made his body prickle as if he'd been filled with electricity.

"Fuck this!" He slapped the towel down on the counter and left the kitchen. Quickly he locked up the house and shut off the lights before heading upstairs.

Tonight, Ayanna. No more running away. No more excuses.

Walking slowly to his son's room, he heard Ayanna's low alto voice as she sang to Devon. "I'll love you forever. I'll like you for always. As long as I'm living. My baby you'll be." A smile appeared on his face as he looked in the bedroom. Ayanna was in the rocking chair near the crib. Devon was basically sound asleep in her arms as she sang.

Back and forth they moved, a faint light shone down and reflected off the book she had long since put down. She'd memorised that story, and he'd often heard her singing the chorus to Devon when he went down for his nap.

As he watched her fingers gently caress Devon's face he stepped in the room. "Hey," he whispered. "Is he out?"

"Yes." she replied softly.

Michael took him and lay him down in the crib. Then he took a hold of Ayanna and led her out of the room. His strong hand cupped her face.

"Stay with me tonight."

Chapter Four

Ayanna looked into his eyes as his words registered, part command and part question. His gaze was direct and unwavering as he watched her. She looked at his nose and lips before returning to his eyes. Instead of verbally giving him an answer, she turned her head until her lips were against the palm of his hand. Lightly, she kissed it as her own hand rested behind his.

His eyes closed before he reached for her and lifted her off her feet. Backing her into the wall, he kissed her. She shivered at the barely restrained passion coiled within his powerful body. *I won't back out this time.*

"Michael," she moaned into his mouth. Her body tensed with hungry anticipation.

"Ayanna," he said on a purr of pleasure as her tongue danced with his. His strong fingers dug into her ass as her legs locked around his waist.

She slid her fingers through his short hair, trying to get as close as possible. Her back pressed against the wall as Michael's wicked mouth teased the satin smooth skin of her neck. A whimper escaped her as his teeth grazed top of her bra before he licked the cleft between her overly sensitive breasts.

Suddenly he stopped. "Not against the wall," he muttered. His voice deeper and more gravelly than normal. "I want you in bed. Not just any bed. *My* bed.

"Yes. Your bed." She pulled his earlobe into her mouth and grazed it with her teeth. He shivered with pleasure. Michael stepped away from the wall and headed to his room.

Ayanna threaded her fingers through his soft hair. Her mouth nipped then licked away the sting along his jaw line. Breathing grew harsher the closer he got to his room. Each step ground her pelvis against him. Their lips met as the remaining distance was covered quickly.

As soon as her feet touched the floor, Michael pulled up her shirt and tossed it to the floor.

"Yours, too," she murmured. Her plea turned into a groan of longing the second his shirt joined hers on the carpet. Moisture pooled between her legs. She could look at him forever and never get bored.

His well-defined chest was rock solid. A light dusting of dark hair scattered over his broad torso. Each cut of muscle on him was a work of art. He didn't have an ounce of extra fat on him.

Sucking her lower lip into her mouth, she closed the miniscule distance between them and ran her fingers over the rippling planes of his upper body. Closing her eyes, she was taken back in time to that night in New Mexico when she had first learned his body. In the years that had passed, her mind hadn't forgotten. His eyes were molten as they opened to stare into hers as her fingers followed the hair that disappeared below the waist of his jeans.

Not moving her gaze from his, she unbuttoned his jeans and lowered the zipper. "Michael," she mouthed as his pants fell around his lean hips. He just watched her, letting her touch him.

Michael's whole body was on fire as her gaze zeroed in on the bulge in his boxers. He wanted to strip her of all her clothes and reclaim her body. When she sucked his lip into her mouth, his cock twitched so painfully in his pants, he thought he might lose control. Somehow, he managed to let her continue her quest.

His pants fell to the floor and he stepped from them, leaving him in his boxers and nothing else. His whole body tensed with the need for the woman before him. His wife. The mother of his child. His Ayanna. His.

That did it. His control snapped faster than a jet catapulted off the deck of an aircraft carrier. He growled low in his throat as he swept her back into his arms.

He placed her gently on the bed and rose up over her. "I've waited a long time for this." He reached out, undid and pulled her shorts down her silken legs. *My God, she's stunning.* He stared at Ayanna. She lay on his bed in bra and panties. He used one hand and opened the front clasp of her white bra and let her breasts fall free. "So beautiful," he mumbled.

His hands lingered along the top of her panties. For all his desperation to be inside her, he wanted to savour this moment.

"Michael." Her eyes held his. "Please."

He pulled her panties down, his fingertips teasing her skin. Michael tossed her underwear to the side. This was how he wanted her. Naked.

His erection swelled even more as he looked at her body. *Stop looking and start acting.* She was the epitome of perfection in his eyes. Faint stretch marks streaked her belly. Her belly was no longer perfectly flat but he didn't care. Her breasts were fuller. "So beautiful," he whispered before he leaned over and kissed her belly.

Ayanna shivered beneath his lips. Michael retraced the small pattern surrounding her belly button and dipped his tongue into it. She whimpered and tossed on the bed.

Michael trailed his lips over her exposed skin. Up one side and down the other of her body. He refused to let her pull him where she wanted him and he avoided the damp lips at the junction of her thighs. He took his time in his homage to her body.

Her cries grew louder. Her hands reached blindly for him as she squirmed on the bedspread.

After blowing gently on her pussy, he licked it. Once. Twice. Three times. Running his thick tongue up between the bald lips. Michael sucked her clit into his mouth and hummed. Lick. Suck. Lick. Suck. He never gave up.

Her body arched off the bed as her hoarse cry filled the room. "Oh shit, Michael!" The hand that landed on the back of his head pressed his face closer to her throbbing entrance. "Don't stop. Please. Please, Michael!" Her fingers dug into the back of his skull as her hips ground her dripping pussy on his lapping tongue. As he ate all she offered him, her grip on him changed and he felt her trying to pull him up her body.

"Tell me, Ayanna. Tell me." Michael rose over her and settled between her spread legs. The head of his erection poised to slide into her wet depth.

"Michael. Please." Her hips arched, trying to force the contact between them.

"Tell me," he insisted.

"Make love to me."

As his hips moved him deep into her velvet heat, a fleeting thought of protection crossed his mind. It vanished as her body moulded itself around him like a long lost lover. "Yes," he hissed as he kissed her, sharing everything he couldn't find the words to say at that moment.

Two halves of the same whole had been brought together again. He could never find another woman who'd made him feel like this again. Each touch from Ayanna's hands, each look from her stunning eyes made him swear he was invincible. She was his soul mate, and while he may have ignored that the first time, he wasn't about to this time.

They moved in perfect harmony, each of them giving and receiving equal pleasure. That pleasure was heightened by the fact they were in each other's arms again.

The room was filled with the sounds of lovers who had been reunited. Moans, groans, mewling, and grunts. Like it had been that night in the hotel their passion for one another flew off the charts. As they expressed their love for one another everything else faded away into nothing. There was no tomorrow, no future, only the current pleasures they shared with each other.

He tucked his beautiful wife closer to his body and kissed the top of her head. "I'm not letting you go this time. I was stupid to allow it the first time. We're a family. You, me and Devon." His arms tightened around her as he thought about her leaving him. "You are my family. Mine."

Ayanna mumbled something unintelligible against his chest, but when her arms tightened around him, he smiled. Not exactly a declaration of love from her, but it wasn't a negative response.

Outside the bedroom window, a star shot across the sky. *Let her love me like I love her*, he wished. "I love you, Ayanna." His eyes shut and he let sleep win the battle.

* * * *

He woke alone. For a brief moment, he thought it may have all been a dream. "No, that wasn't a dream, was it?" he murmured, sitting up in bed. He couldn't see any signs that she'd been there. Flopping back, he groaned. If it was just a dream, he was screwed. He laid there for a moment, then got up, slipped on some pants and headed downstairs.

A sigh of relief left him as he saw Devon on his three-wheeler going as fast as he could and squealing with joy as he headed into the living room. On his heels was…Racer.

As Devon headed around the couch and back into the kitchen, Michael met his friend's gaze.

"Morning, Taz," Racer said with a smirk as he took in the shirtless man on the steps.

"What are you doing here?" Michael asked

"We have a long-standing golf game. What? Forget about it?" Racer winked. "Well, I would too, if I got to share my nights with Ayanna."

"Watch it, Kysenzki," Michael warned.

"Da-da!" Devon squealed as he came rolling back into the room.

Michael bent down to pick up Devon and kissed his cheek. Then he set him back upon the seat of his toy. "Morning, sport."

The two men went into the kitchen and Michael's breath caught in his throat. Ayanna had that effect on him. She was talking to her friend Lauren as they made breakfast.

Slowly, he took in the black and white crossover contrast pants she wore for working out. One half of his mouth turned up in a smirk as he noticed she wore one of his shirts. His eyes lingered on her butt as it swayed to the music that played in the kitchen.

"Damn," he muttered before striding across the kitchen and sweeping her into his arms to kiss her.

Ayanna smiled as he kissed her. Placing her arms around his neck, she returned the passionate embrace. "Morning," she said as she wriggled out of his arms and turned her attention back to preparing food.

"Morning," he responded in a husky voice. "Lauren. Good to see you."

"And you, Michael. Oh, I like this song" She grinned as she looked back at Ayanna and turned up the music. She wore similar clothing to Ayanna. Michael looked over his shoulder at Racer and stepped back, watching the two women in the kitchen dance to the music.

Ayanna set down her knife and picked up Devon, dancing with him and singing. Spinning him around until he laughed uncontrollably.

Family. My family. Michael smiled.

Racer stepped up next to him and said, "You got it made, man. Don't fuck this up. That is one special woman you have there."

"I'm beginning to realise just how special," Michael agreed in a low tone as the women continued to have a wonderful time.

* * * *

Ayanna couldn't dwell on Michael. She had to study for her finals. Her husband and Racer were off playing golf. Lauren was downstairs playing with Devon. Ayanna couldn't waste time.

Despite how wonderful it had been to be back in Michael's arms, she was determined not to succumb to her desire again. She had to focus on her schooling and her son *not* how good being with Michael was. With him gone with his friend, her body had a momentary reprieve from the temptation wrapped in the sinful package called Lieutenant Michael Kelly Taylor. That arrogant pilot, amazing father, husband, and wonderful lover had the power to distract her from her goals and she couldn't let that happen.

She opened her books. Last night with Michael had been amazing, but now her studies had first priority. Immersing herself, it hardly registered when Lauren came to tell her Michael was back and she was leaving. A few hours later, Ayanna closed the book and groaned. Rolling her shoulders, she rubbed her eyes. She pushed away from the desk and went to check on Devon who was napping.

She froze when she heard voices coming from downstairs.

She recognised Michael's voice and the other sounded familiar. Feminine and high pitched. Ayanna wrapped her arms around her middle as it clicked. This was the woman who'd waylaid Michael on base the day he'd landed back into her life. Bridget or something like that.

Ayanna knew better than to eavesdrop, but she couldn't bring herself to give them privacy. Deep fear settled in her gut. Close on its heels was jealousy.

"I know Papa will be so happy that we're a couple," Bridget's voice carried to Ayanna's ears.

"We aren't a couple, Bridget. I told you that a long time ago. I'm sorry you and your mother believe we should be. I'm not available," Michael said.

Ayanna began to walk down the stairs. A calculating gleam appeared in Bridget's eyes as she saw her.

"But, Michael, I'm pregnant. About seven weeks...and...oh, I didn't know you had a guest." Bridget covered her mouth and tried to look embarrassed.

Michael turned around and met Ayanna's gaze.

She forced herself to maintain a bland expression. "Don't mind me," she said softly. "I'm just going to the kitchen."

He followed her. "Ayanna, wait," he insisted.

"No, Michael. I'd say you have something important to discuss with that woman." She waved him off and walked to the fridge to grab a bottled water before heading back upstairs.

I knew this was too good to be true.

Minutes later, she heard the door slam and feet pounding up the stairs. Taking a drink of her water, she gathered her inner strength and waited for her door to open.

She didn't have long to wait. Michael swung it open without even knocking. "Let me explain."

"I don't think I need an explanation. I'm fully aware of how that works. I was there. Although I found out at eight weeks, but still." She shrugged, determined not to show how hurt she was.

"She's lying. Well, perhaps not about being pregnant, but if she is, it isn't mine." Michael shut the door behind him and walked over to stand in front of her.

Ayanna kept her eyes on water bottle in her hand. "Whatever. As long as you don't try and gyp Devon of anything, what you do is your business." She understood that the part of her prone to ruining good things was rearing its ugly head.

"What are you saying?" he demanded as the bottle was removed from her hand and he forced an eye connection.

"We both know the only reason you married me was for convenience. And I appreciate what you've done for me and Devon. But—"

His eyes grew hard as ice and colder than that. "Shut up, Ayanna. Don't even go down that fucking road. This marriage is a marriage not a goddamn convenience." He clenched his jaw. "Maybe at first, in the beginning." He relaxed and a brief grin flashed across his face. "No, not even then. I've always known I wanted something more from you."

"No, it's wrong." Her heart swelled at what she heard. *Could he be for real?*

"What's wrong about it, Ayanna?" Exasperation slammed full force back into his voice. "I'll give you this, it started off in a unique way, but," he took her hands, "it's real now. This. You. Me. Devon. This is real. *We* are a family."

"And Bridget?" Ayanna recognised the desperation in her voice. But, she had to know.

"That was just Bridget being Bridget. I have never even screwed her."

Her eyes searched his. *He seems so certain about what he says. Why can't I believe him?* "I just don't know," she protested.

"What? What are you doubting? And why? The fact I was stupid to leave you that first night? And that you think I'm doing this because I feel guilty about you having to struggle with Devon for a few years? You're right, I do feel guilty. I should have been there. I should have married you that night. Part of me wanted to." She swallowed as he took her hands. "Marrying you has never been a regret. Ever. I love Devon." He made sure she couldn't pull away. "And I love you."

Her belly filled with butterflies. *He loves me.* She drew her bottom lip into her mouth. *I can't say it yet. I...I...I just can't.*

She pulled a hand free from his hold and trailed it down the side of his face before gathering his shirt below his Adam's apple. "Good," she ground out. "The next hussy who comes to the door and claims that, is gonna get her ass beat. Clear?"

Michael smiled as he kissed her. "Yes, my wife. Understood." Standing, he pulled her against his broad chest. He glanced at the book of American poets, he had seen in that purple purse the day his life had changed for the better. "Now, do you have time...for *your husband* or do you have more studying to do?"

Time for my husband? So much for no repeats of sleeping with him. She tilted her head. *Was that why he said he loved me?*

Her pussy clenched. *Oh, to hell with it. I want him.* "Well," she purred as her hands slid around his waist. "I could study you, you know, perhaps do a little art appreciation." She licked her lips and demurely lowered her lashes.

"Little? A *little* art appreciation?" he growled as he bent her backwards and nibbled on her jaw line.

"I believe that was the word I used. But...care to prove me wrong?" Her fingers dug into his corded forearms as he bent her further.

"Oh, hell yeah. We'll see how *little* you think he is."

"Such talk." Lifting her head, Ayanna met his gaze. "Just take me to bed, Michael."

"Yes, my beautiful wife. I think I should take you to bed. Then you can apologise to him for calling him little."

Ayanna held his gaze as her hands untied the drawstring on his shorts and pushed them down. "You're right," she cooed. "I should apologise."

Michael muttered incoherently.

Her hands held his erection. "You know, you were right about something else." She dropped to her knees. "He's not little at all." Fingers stroked along the length. "It's like velvet over iron."

"Ayanna."

"Hush. I'm apologising." She kissed the head of his dick, smiling as it leapt in response. "I'm sorry." Her mouth engulfed it, tongue swiping across the top, cleaning away the pre-cum.

Settling more comfortably on her knees, she began to slide him in and out of her mouth. "Ah hell, Ayanna," he groaned from above her.

One hand rested upon a corded thigh while the other reached between his legs to tease his balls. Her wet mouth slipped up and down. She removed her mouth and wrapped her hands back around him, cradling him between her soft palms. Stroking him up and down, moving easy with her saliva that was there.

"Fuck. I want to come." His voice grated.

"Shhh. I'm not done with my apology." One hand fisted around him and moved faster while her gaze remained focused on the cock before her. *Everything on him is beautiful.*

He moaned, fists clenching, hips beginning to thrust. "I'm about to come."

Licking her lips, she put the head of his dick back in her mouth, her tongue ran along the edge. She tightened the circle her hand made near the base and began milking him.

A deep growl erupted as thick, salty ejaculate filled her mouth. Michael pumped his hips as he came furiously in her mouth.

When there was no more to swallow, she sat back and grinned at him. "I hope he accepts my apology."

Michael stared at her. He couldn't do anything else. Ayanna licked her lips as if she'd just finished the most scrumptious sundae. She looked up at him with those sexy brown eyes, that saucy grin and a look of such satisfaction on her face.

His cock twitched as his eyes moved over her still-moist lips. The tops of her breasts tempted him. Even her ears tempted him. *I am the luckiest man in the world.*

He assisted her up off the floor and kissed her. His tongue swept like a river through her mouth. Stepping out of his shorts, he lifted her, placing her legs around his waist. He walked to the door and shut it before returning to Ayanna's bed.

He dropped her on the bed. Her eyes widened as she bounced. He groaned as her breasts jiggled inside her shirt. He jerked his shirt off, tossing it to the side. "Get your sexy body on your hands and knees."

"What?" Her question floated through the air.

"You heard me. Hands and knees and stay by the end of the mattress. I wanna see that ass in the air." His order was sharp. He noticed an immediate flush to her skin. Her plump lips parted with excitement.

Ayanna did as he ordered. Stroking one hand along his hard-on, he lifted her skirt and groaned. She wore no panties. "You are such a naughty wench. No panties. Jesus, Ayanna," he mumbled, "your pussy is so wet."

He rested her skirt on the small of her back, exposing her totally to him. One finger teased her cleft as he continued to move closer to his own piece of heaven. As his finger moved, she looked at him over her shoulder and blinked once. A slow blink before facing forward.

Michael ran the head of his cock between her lips, drenching it with her juices. He thrust once and sheathed himself totally within her.

"Oh my God!" she wailed as her head dropped towards the mattress.

"Come on my cock, baby," he ordered. He drilled into her faster and faster. He shut his eyes on the sight of her ass shaking in front of him as his balls tightened. He pounded harder. The walls of her tight pussy clenched around him as she climaxed.

A roar erupted from him as he exploded inside her. Sweat ran from his body to hers as his limbs shook. He collapsed on her, pressing her body into the mattress while they fought to regain their breath. Then he pulled out and moved them up further on the bed to spoon them together.

* * * *

Fifteen minutes later, Michael stood under the spray of the shower head. Fabulous memories of making love to her filled his mind as he turned off the water. He had to get her into his bedroom. He wanted it all with Ayanna. Not just snatches of her love. As he dried off, he ran through how to tell her. Pulling on a pair of clean khakis, he looked in the mirror. *I know she responds to me, but how does she truly feel about me? How can I be so sure about my feelings and yet she seems so hesitant?*

He ran the towel over his short hair then reached for a black shirt and tugged it over his head. Hanging up his towel then leaving the bathroom, he went downstairs still trying to figure out what he was going to do about his wife.

Chapter Five

Michael smiled with the rush he felt as his F/A-18 Super Hornet took to the sky. He loved it up here. Was it possible for life to get any better? Being a pilot was...indescribable.

"You okay up there, Taz?" Racer asked from behind. "You're awfully quiet."

"Just enjoying the view, Racer. Just enjoying the view."

"Sure you are. You're probably trying to come up with some way to get that wife of yours up here and inducted into the mile-high club."

Male laughter reached his ears and Michael knew the rest of the squadron was listening in. They'd all surprised him and Ayanna last week when they'd stopped by his home to meet his wife and son. They'd come with their significant others and families, bringing food and a cake. Michael had been very pleased at how welcoming they'd been to Ayanna and Devon.

Now that it was just the guys, it was time for the ribbing to begin anew. They'd already been merciless to him when they'd found out he'd kept Ayanna a secret from them.

"Well, if I thought there was a way to accomplish that in this cockpit, I'd sure do it," Michael retorted. An image of Ayanna naked in his plane impaled on his cock was a helluva erotic image to him. Her juices coating his erection as he took them to new planes of pleasure was something even his jet couldn't deliver. Michael shifted as his penis swelled.

"Sure she wouldn't prefer the stick your hands are on?" Racer teased. "Or rather, the one it should be on."

"Watch it, Racer. He's liable to get so excited thinking about her, y'all will crash," another voice broke in.

"Don't be jealous that you still have to pay for women, Coyote," Michael retorted. Racer snorted behind him.

Their conversation halted as they received their orders and began their flight op. The second they'd succeeded and were heading back to base, the ribbing began again. Michael took it all with good cheer — until a voice broke in.

It wiped all the cheer from their faces. They had a mission and were needed out at sea. As one, the small squadron of three planes headed out over the Atlantic Ocean to the aircraft carrier where they'd refuel and receive their new orders.

As the F/A-18's shot across the blue sky and headed from home, Michael wondered how Ayanna would take this new development.

The men chatted amongst themselves. Michael looked on either side of him and nodded at the men there. He had the best men with him. There were no others he'd rather have at his side. Their tactical precision was unmatched by anyone which was precisely the reason they'd been sent on this mission.

It was dark when they landed on the flight deck of the carrier. After checking in with the ship's Commanding

Officer, the men got briefed on their mission. They'd leave in a few hours but first they needed to get some food and sleep.

Michael nodded to his men as they went to their temporary quarters or the mess. Personally, he had a call to make. He wanted to explain things to Ayanna. He also craved the soothing sound of her voice.

Michael stood by a ship to shore phone and stared. "Would you like some privacy, Lieutenant?" the CO asked as he stopped beside him. "Rumour has it you're recently married. Congratulations."

"Thank you, sir. And yes, if you don't mind, I would love some privacy."

"Very good, stop by my stateroom, and I'll let you use my phone." The CO patted him on the back and walked off.

Michael followed him immediately, wanting desperately to hear Ayanna's voice. Soon he was looking at the white receiver of the MRSAT in the CO's stateroom. He picked it up then set it back down again. He was scared. He had heard horror stories from other sailors about what had happened between them and their spouses when deployed. Infidelity. Spitefulness.

He shook his head. *Ayanna isn't like that.*

Finally he just dialled his home number and held his breath as the phone began to ring.

"Lieutenant Taylor's residence," Ayanna answered in her smooth alto tone. Just her voice managed to soothe his nerves.

"Hey, Ayanna," Michael said over the static-filled line.

"Michael? Where are you? You sound scratchy."

"I'm not coming home for a while," he told her. The static grew then faded. "Okay? I'm on a mission."

He waited for a response and got nothing.

"Ayanna? Honey, are you there?"

Nothing.

The call had been lost.

Michael dropped the phone back on its cradle and swore as he stood up. When he opened the door, the CO was waiting. "Everything okay at home, Lieutenant?"

"We got disconnected, but thank you, Sir, for letting me use your phone." Michael sent him a tense smile and walked off.

I am so totally fucked. I don't even know how much she heard.

* * * *

Ayanna hung up the phone, oblivious to the tears streaming down her face. *Not coming home for a while.* Well, that explained why he still wasn't home at eleven o'clock at night.

He doesn't want to be with you anymore, her mind taunted. She swallowed, no, that couldn't be right. *Why not? You gave him what he wanted, sex. That's all men ever want.*

Refusing to let her mind continue down that destructive road, she tried to turn her attention back to the task at hand. Studying.

It wasn't easy. The words from her notes and books seemed to mock her very being. She saw Michael's face in them. "Damn it!" Her hand smacked the desk as she struggled to get her work done. "I don't have time for this. I *have* to study. That hands-on practical is just around the corner."

It was near two when she finally gave in and crawled into bed, wearing one of Michael's shirts. He'd left it in her room one night when he'd had come to her—something that had irked him. He wanted her to share his room, but she still refused. It looked like he was tired of walking down the hall.

"Get a grip, Ayanna," she admonished herself as she rolled over and punched her pillow. "Don't assume anything."

Still, sleep eluded her until she allowed her fingers to drift between her thighs, along with an image of the man who'd defined passion for her.

* * * *

Her state of mind didn't improve. Life without Michael was hard. Very hard. Each passing day sent her mind down roads she knew in her heart were best left untravelled, but unfortunately they were frequented on an hourly basis.

She received calls from the significant others of the men who flew with Michael. They left messages which said to call if she needed anything, *anything* at all. Ayanna was grateful for the kindness but she didn't call. Between working, school, and Devon she stayed almost busy enough to keep his image at bay.

Almost.

Still she hurried to the phone each time it rang only to be disappointed when it wasn't him.

Lauren did her best to explain how things worked in the military. She rationalised he'd most likely been disconnected and Ayanna hadn't heard all he'd wanted to say. Ayanna didn't know what to think. She wanted desperately to believe Lauren, but her mind kept coming up with vicious reasons for his absence.

Matters weren't helped by Devon constantly running around crying "Da-da". He didn't understand why Michael wasn't there and began to act out.

One night, two weeks after Michael had gone, the phone finally rang. Exhausted from working extra hours and from her studies, Ayanna wanted nothing but her bed. Sinking into the leather chair beside the phone, she answered wearily, "Lieutenant Taylor's residence."

"Ayanna? Baby is that you? Can you hear me?" Michael's rich voice reached across the line and threaded itself deep in her system — a system that still desperately craved him.

"Hello, Michael," she said softly as tears filled her eyes.

"I can't talk long but I wanted to see how you and Devon are doing. Is everything okay?"

"We're both fine. Thanks for asking." The traitorous tears leaked down her face. His comforting voice broke through the shell she'd erected to keep her sanity.

"Ayanna?" he asked. "What's wrong?"

She fought down a sniff as another rush of unexpected emotions swarmed her. *I have to keep strong. I can't be weak.* "I'm fine. Devon's doing well. How are you?" She heard the impersonal edge to her tone. Part of her longed to give in and cry but her pride demanded she stay and act strong.

"I'm okay. I miss you," he paused. "Are you sure everything is fine at home?"

"Yes, I'm sure. Thanks for calling and letting me know how you were doing. Stay safe. Goodbye, Michael." She replaced the cordless phone on the base and headed for bed.

* * * *

Michael looked at the phone like a foreign object. The droning of the dial tone reached him. She'd hung up. Just like that. Just a short goodbye and then...nothing. Her tone...so distant.

He replaced the receiver and wiped a hand down his face. He felt devastated. They really hadn't ever talked about what being a Navy wife was going to be like. Every time he tried to bring up his job, she'd found a way to change the subject. She still kept a barrier between them. Sure, at night it was different, but she refused to share his room like a true married couple.

"Ayanna," he mumbled as he left to go back to his quarters. Racer was in there when he walked in.

"You alright there, Taz?"

"Pete, man, I don't know what to do. I'm torn." Michael sat down heavily on his bunk.

"Wow, it must be serious. Look man, we're supposed to be going home tomorrow. You'll go home, take her in your arms and kiss the hell out of her. Sometime later, after you're done loving her, you'll explain how things are as a pilot's wife." Racer sent him an encouraging smile. "It'll work out. Where's your faith?"

Lying on his back, Michael looked at the ceiling. "I don't know. She sounded so distant, dispassionate even." Closing his eyes, he thought over his mission. They had flown over parts of South America to 'tactically erase' some terrorists that had gathered there, and they'd managed to do so without any other civilian causalities. But his mind still wandered back to Ayanna.

He needed to know that Ayanna understood his job and what it meant. Michael needed to know that she didn't think he was out sleeping with anyone else. "I need her to know I love her and Devon."

Laughter reached him and he opened his eyes and saw Racer standing over him. "Tell her man. Just tell her."

"You're right." Michael sat up and saw his two wingmen and their RIO's looking at him as well. "Get outta here guys. Grab some sleep, we're haulin' ass home tomorrow."

The remaining crew waved and went to their own bunks. Michael went to sleep dreaming about Ayanna and Devon. The next afternoon when they launched from the flight deck a familiar rush went to his bones. At the same time, an extra one that told him he was soon going to be with his wife.

* * * *

The next day, work dragged on and on. Ayanna was exhausted from her restless night.

Her dreams had been haunted. She and Michael were kept separate by a chasm, a chasm that only grew each time she reached for him. By the time she'd woken, covered in sweat, the distance between them had grown from the size of a crack in the pavement to larger than the Grand Canyon, or so it seemed to her heavy heart.

Additionally, she was tense about hearing back on the practical exams that she'd taken, and all she wanted was get home to her son. It was a relief to finally walk through the door with Devon. At home, there was no need to pretend everything was alright. She let Devon play while she decided what to do about dinner. A picnic would be fun, but it would have to be inside since a late afternoon storm had rolled into the area.

She spread out a vinyl tablecloth on the floor and she sat on it with Devon to enjoy a fun dinner of finger foods. She watched her son build something out of cheese slices and grapes.

"Well, Devon. I'm done. Mama is almost a pharmacist. What do you think about that?" Ayanna asked as she dunked a carrot stick in some dip and ate it.

Big soulful eyes looked up at her and he grinned. Wrinkling his nose, he placed one finger across his lips, his sign for 'quiet.' Seconds after that, cheese squished between his fingers as he blew kisses to the room, his new, favourite thing to do.

Just as she grinned at his antics, he exclaimed, "Da-da."

Dropping her head, she muttered, "Figures. That *would* be your answer. No love for mama."

"Da-da!" he said again as he pushed from his seat on the floor.

"I don't think he wants that piece of cheese. Eat your food." She directed a wayward piece of cheese back to Devon's mouth. "Not to mention your Da-da isn't here right now."

A deep masculine voice filled the kitchen. "Actually he is. And for the record, I would love a piece of cheese and am very proud that you're almost a pharmacist."

Devon giggled as Ayanna jumped. The happy child ran to the gate she'd had put to keep him and the food in the kitchen. She turned in time to see Michael pick him up.

He was home!

Michael kissed Devon and stepped over the baby gate. "Hello, Ayanna."

It was almost surreal. Her gaze travelled over him as he stood there in his flight suit. She noticed a slight hesitation or even fear in his eyes as his dark brown gaze stared back at her. Almost as if he was unsure of her reaction.

I love him.

Ayanna smiled as the realisation hit her. She loved him. And he loved her.

True, there were many things they had to discuss, things she couldn't continue to run away from. The life of a military wife, more specifically a pilot's wife. *Because, that's what I am. A US Navy pilot's wife.*

Finally getting up off the floor, she walked towards him as he held their child and looked so devastatingly handsome. He took her breath away.

"Hi," she managed to mumble.

One strong arm reached out and pulled her to his body. Their lips met and even Devon's rambles faded into the background.

* * * *

Upon arrival at NAS Oceana the foul weather had delayed landing a tiny bit. Michael had sent his wingmen in first, making sure they'd gotten down safely before he'd taken himself out of the sky.

Farewells had been brief as he'd had the craving to get home and see his family. Rushing home, he'd parked his vehicle and run to the house, where he'd let himself in. He'd dropped his bag in the entryway and he listened for Devon and Ayanna.

He'd easily pinpointed their location in the kitchen and hurried to join them. Standing behind the baby gate, he'd taken in the scene. The table was off to the side, and Ayanna had placed a tablecloth down on the floor.

Her back had been to him, so his eyes had travelled over her, soaking up the vision she offered in a pale green tank top and dark grey pants.

His son had seen him and immediately Michael had put his finger across his lips. An action that Devon had mimicked before blowing kisses and chortling, "Da-da." Michael had blinked back tears at the love in Devon's eyes.

The moment he'd spoken and Ayanna had turned to look at him, Michael had known he'd come home for good. This was what life was all about.

As he kissed his wife, he thanked God she was still here. "We have to talk." *I love her so much!*

"I know." She snuggled closer to him, her arms slipping around his waist.

Michael kissed the top of her head and then bounced Devon in his arm. "And how was he while I was gone?"

"Difficult," she answered. "Have you eaten?"

"No. We landed and I came home as soon as I could." He ran his hand up her exposed arm. "I'm starving though," he said, his deep tone full of another meaning. He knew she could feel his swollen cock pressing into her side.

Her body shuddered with arousal.

"Let me go change and I'll be right back," he said.

He took Devon with him upstairs, chatting about he expected him to behave better the next time da-da was gone.

He changed into grey Navy sweats and a blue shirt while Devon laughed and talked up a storm. In no time, he was on his way back downstairs.

The gentle strands of IL DIVO played through the room. Ayanna sang along to the song, *Amour Venme A Buscar.*

As they sat back down on the floor to eat, he reached across the space separating them and took her hand. When her lighter eyes met his, he swallowed. "I love you, Ayanna."

Her eyes grew big. "What?"

Michael manoeuvred to kneel before her. He cupped her face in his large hands. "I love you. I. Love. You."

"I love you, too, Michael. I love you, too."

A growl of satisfaction erupted from his throat as he lifted her to straddle his lap. "Do you know how much I've longed to hear those words from your mouth?"

"I love you," she said over and over as their mouths met with a blinding passion. Her stomach grumbled. Loudly. She pulled back from him and tucked her head into his neck.

"Hungry, dear?" he asked with a chuckle. *As much as I want to make love to her, just being with her is more than perfect.*

"Starved."

"Guess that means I should set you down, so we can get to the meal."

"I suppose," She replied, disappointment heavy in her tone.

Reluctantly he set her beside him and they began to eat. After a few moments, he spoke. "You do know we aren't having separate rooms anymore, don't you?"

She laughed. "I hope not. I've missed you."

"When is Devon's bedtime again?" Michael asked.

"Not for a while," she responded as she trailed one finger along his jaw.

He shivered at her simple touch. "Keep that up, and he'll be going to bed much earlier than normal."

"Impatient?"

"You have no idea," he said.

"Good. Now, eat up."

"I plan on it." Picking up a carrot stick, he offered it to her. "You're gonna need your energy."

"Really? So pilots can go for a long time?" Her thick lashes fluttered.

"This one can," he growled. "And I've never failed to deliver."

Laughing, they both ate and enjoyed just being together until they could reunite in the way their bodies craved. Later, as Michael watched his wife put their son down for the night, everything about her called to him.

His gaze lingered over the way her full hips moved when she walked. How her breasts seemed to almost spill out of her shirt, but manage to look classy at the same time. Ayanna Genat Taylor was all he could ever want and more. If he had thought doing 7Gs in his jet sent him spinning, then from now on, it wouldn't affect him. The woman in his arms affected him much more than that.

As she shut Devon's door behind her, he pulled her close. Trailing his lips along the skin of her neck, he grew hard as the taste of her skin filled his mouth. "I want to love you."

He lifted her and carried her easily down the darkened hall to his bedroom.

Ayanna shivered.

The pleasure which erupted within her simply by being held close to his chest was mind-blowing. The deeply sexual tone he spoke in warmed her to the point of being single-handedly capable of melting a polar ice cap.

"Yes," she murmured. "Love me, Michael."

A slow seductive smile crossed his face as he closed the door behind them, creating the private sanctuary she longed for.

"All night long, baby," he promised. He set her down, searing her with the explosive heat in his gaze. "First things first. Let's get rid of these clothes."

Ayanna missed his touch the second he set her down. She whimpered softly and was blessed by another wicked grin from the tall man before her.

His callused hands skated up her bare arms to her collarbone. She trembled as her sensitive nipples tightened with anticipation. He unbuttoned her sleeveless blouse, slipping it off her shoulders. Without a word, one strong hand reached around her ribcage and expertly undid her bra.

As her breasts tumbled free of their confinement, she muttered, "Well now, that seemed mightily practiced."

She loved the blush that graced his face at her comment.

Her belly quivered as he knelt before her, his warm breath dancing along her exposed skin. His long fingers examined her stomach. Ayanna tipped her head and watched the myriad emotions on his face as he touched her. Pleasured her.

His hair shone in the room's soft light, the summer sun having given his normally dark hair lighter streaks. She watched the way his straight white teeth sank into his bottom lip, how his head cocked to the side as his eyes followed the path his fingers travelled.

She swallowed hard as he moved down over the swell of her hips to the button that rested on her right hip. Every action was smooth, seemingly effortless — even the way he lowered the zipper of her pants and drew them off her legs.

Ayanna knew he could smell her arousal, hell she could. She didn't care, she wanted him to touch her. "Michael," she stuttered as his index finger ran along the edge of her satin thong.

"Damn it, Ayanna. I wanted to go slow, make love to you as you deserve, but," his hands gripped her hips and pulled her close so her dripping pussy was right before his mouth, "sitting here, smelling your scent. I want to rip this fucking purple thong off and screw you until neither of us can think."

Dropping one hand to rest on the back of his head, Ayanna urged him closer. "Don't hear me complaining, do you?"

Her other hand manoeuvred between her crotch and his face, she slid her fingers under the wet material, allowing them to sink into her. Moving them up and down until they were wet with her juices, Ayanna removed them from her pussy and put them to his lips.

Michael's mouth sucked on her fingers until there was no more taste for him to get from them. He nudged her thong out of the way and began feasting on her.

Her moans quickly turned to loud mews of pleasure. Somehow, her thong was removed and he kept his mouth pressed hard to her. His thick tongue fucked her until she came.

"Michael!" she cried as her body shook.

He stayed on his knees until he was sure he had gotten it all. When he rose before her, her body pulsed with eagerness at the raw, primal craving she saw. Her eyes drifted down to the obvious ridge in his sweatpants. She licked her lips. *I want to suck on that cock.*

Michael lowered his pants and whipped off his shirt. She shifted as she tried to keep her moisture inside her body as opposed to leaking down her leg. His naked body made her lust uncontrollably. All of him was magnificent, but she focused on the thick cock that jutted out from the nest of dark hair.

Again, she wet her lips and reached for him. She groaned in tandem with him as her fingers closed about him. Her pussy pumped and sent another orgasm through her. She loved the feel of him in her hand.

Leaning forward, she took him in her mouth. His moan made her smile. He gripped her hair and gently tugged her away from him. Confused, Ayanna looked up at him. *What does he want?* The answer was on his face. He needed her.

"I need to be inside you, Ayanna. I need to feel your pussy around my cock." His words were husky with strain.

She nodded. She stood and walked to the bed, sitting down on it and holding out her hand towards the handsome lieutenant who happened to be her husband. Hers.

Michael followed her. He settled between her legs. She helped guide him inside her and they both caught their breath at the sensation of being joined in such a way.

Eyes on each other, he began to slowly move inside her. The rhythm quickly gave way to a faster, deeper, harder thrusting of hips. Ayanna screamed herself hoarse as her hips rose to meet each powerful stroke.

Throughout the night, they made love. They explored each other's bodies. Ayanna sat up and looked at her husband in the gentle light of morning. Thick lashes rested on his cheeks as he slumbered. He lay on his back, the sage-coloured sheet resting just below his navel. Her eyes travelled over his bared chest, admiring the masculine form.

"My husband," she mumbled.

Tugging down the sheet, she exposed his cock to her gaze. She licked her lips. Reaching out, she touched it gently, slowly running her fingers up the shaft. She never stopped watching as it grew harder and stiffer in her grasp.

Low grunts and groans came from Michael as he continued to sleep. His hips shifted a bit and Ayanna rose up on the bed. Carefully, she straddled him and sank down his aroused shaft. Her body trembled as he filled her. She closed her eyes, tipped back her head and began to move upon him.

"Now, this is a wonderful way to wake up," his sleep-laden voice said.

Ayanna didn't stop riding him but she did look down at him. "I couldn't agree more." She smiled as his hands landed on her hips and he began to move opposite her, so when she came down, he went up, allowing much deeper penetration.

Her nails scored over his naked chest as she neared her release. His rumbles offset her mewls. Up and down she moved, rotating her hips, angling them so he hit different spots inside her.

"Oh God," she moaned as her entire body began to tingle. Michael took her hands in his and laced their fingers together. She came in a rush and collapsed on top of him, panting hard.

Michael rolled her so he was on top, their joined hands above her head. His hips continued to pump into her. "You were made for me, baby. I fit so perfectly inside you. I love you."

She could see the sweat on his skin, feel the pounding of his heart. "I love you, too," she said on a low purr of satisfaction.

Hooking her ankles so her feet rested on his back, Ayanna closed her eyes again and gave herself over to the pleasure this man brought her.

This was where she belonged.

IN THE ARMS
OF A PILOT

Jennah Sharpe

Dedication

For George.

Chapter One

1941 came in with a bang. Popping champagne bottles and crackers littered the night with noise. We celebrated New Year's with a flourish at the Jump Club on Broad Street. Streamers, glitter and confetti covered the floor in a slippery blanket. Crowds of wives and girlfriends clung to their army men, under the pervasive cloud of cigarette smoke, as if their very willpower could keep the boys safe.

My own RAF pilot was dapper in his starched army-green uniform and all the girls watched him, waiting perhaps for me to leave. That was more than likely. He was the most handsome man in the club. I wanted to be anywhere but the Jump Club with it's glassy, polished floors and exuberant jive. It really wasn't my style, especially that night. While others seemed to be able to lose themselves in the patriotic atmosphere of the night, I could not. A dark, ominous fog obscured my perception and seemed to follow all of us, waiting for its chance to blanket us with despair, even if no one else could see it.

I took William's hand for comfort, relishing the warmth of his nearness. He wrapped his arm around my waist leading me in a rendition of the Blue Danube. Strangely, the lilting waltz, which should have been romantic and uplifting, seemed to me a haunting death knell for both the men in the room and our country as a whole.

The second Great War was never-ending. The German front was advancing, seemingly unstoppable. I was certain the world would be left barren if it continued much longer. There could be no recovery from the horrors of war. The blackout curtains I'd sewn the day after I first met William at the Women's Royal Naval Service dinner and dance were thinning and faded. I needed new ones for the front hall but black material was next to non-existent. I debated using my grandmother's handmade quilt. It was dark navy and thick but I couldn't bring myself to cut it into two pieces as was needed in the hall. I missed eggs, cold milk, driving to the country on weekends and walking with William in the park without fear of a bomb turning us to dust.

I shared my little flat with two other women working for the Women's Royal Naval service, more commonly called Wrens, and we got along famously. Wanda was moving out in two weeks to marry her beau and live with him. Sarah wouldn't be far behind if the noises from her room at night, when her boyfriend dropped by, were any indication.

The flat featured three small bedrooms, a sitting room and a small kitchenette, just the right size for three single girls surviving in London. We did everything together, Sarah, Wanda and I, right down to finding our men at the same time. That dinner dance would remain in my memory until the end of my days. Then, at the height of the war, our carefree days seemed to be ending and so far away all at once. I was in a bit of a limbo, young and lively one day, solemn and old the next.

We'd let the flat out to another group of young women and were packing for the move to be wives to our soldiers. The new girls would take over within the month.

If our society had been a touch more liberal, we would have seen that staying together while our men left for the front would have been a much more stable situation. It didn't do any of us any good to wander about empty flats or houses, worrying when the black edged letter, signalling the demise of a loved husband, would appear in our mail slot.

The Blue Danube wound to a close. Wanda caught my eye and smiled at me. I smiled back, but it was forced. I wanted nothing more than to take William home and never let him leave, but I couldn't say that to anyone. How patriotic would that be? Not to mention it would start an argument between William and I. Tall and grand in his uniform, I wanted him to leave with a smile for me on his face, not words of how I didn't appreciate all that he was doing for his country and the world in general.

Wanda was flashy in her pink sequins; her blonde curls piled high on her head. Her long legs flying to the beat of a campy army song meant to give the men morale, she was completely unaware of the men on the sidelines ogling her. She only had eyes for the man she was engaged to. How ironic that the men were there for any piece of ass they could get their hands on, just to have willing company on their last night in town and here we were, all three of us, committed. The single Wren's were having the time of their lives, and I envied them their innocence, their joy and the lust filled, coy glances they were free to distribute amongst the soldiers. Not that I would have given up William. Don't get me wrong, but to marry a man who was leaving for war seemed a catalyst for bad luck. I could give him the slick honeymoon sex he craved and something to fight for, to come home to, but what did that leave me?

Sarah too, with her red hair curled about her face, seemed to be lost in the music. As I watched her swing around the room, barefoot and light as a feather, envy coursed through me once again, it's thick, green venom winding its way through my veins. How could they be so blind to the danger, to the solitude? Or maybe they weren't. Maybe it was as much a show for their fiancées as my smile was for William. There was no way to know without asking them.

William gave me a nod from the bar, a cold pop in his hand, as if to ask if I wanted anything to drink. I shook my head and sidled up to Wanda who was now resting in a chair against the wall, clapping her hands to the music. I took the empty seat beside her.

"Wanda, I think Will and I are going to head back to the flat," I told her. "You'll take the underground home with Sarah?"

"You're going home already, Emmy? The night is young. You can make out here, you know. No one will notice." She winked. "You don't have to go home." Her green eyes flashed with life. I'd miss her when she left. Both she and Sarah were going to leave a hole in my life, perhaps even more gaping than the hole William would dig with his leaving.

I smiled indulgently. "We want more than what is acceptable here on the dance floor, Wanda. Don't be silly. They've moved up the date for deployment, you know. We're thinking of visiting the judge tomorrow to have him marry us. It would mean having more time together as a married couple. That's important to Will."

"Really? And the date's been moved up?"

"That's what William tells me. Just come in quietly, will you?"

Wanda touched my shoulder. "Of course. I'll tell Sarah and AJ. I'll tell them to keep it down."

That made me laugh. Wanda could always make me laugh under the worst of circumstances. "We should have told them that, months ago. Why should tonight be any different?"

"Huh. You're right. Why did we put up with all that moaning? We should have been competing." She slapped my back. "Doesn't Will make you scream his name?" She winked again.

"Hardly. His lovemaking is soft and quiet." I drew in a breath at the thought, my gaze searching the room for my lover.

"Just like he is, right?" teased Wanda.

"Oh, he's quiet all right, but he's anything but soft."

Wanda laughed out loud again. I smiled. This time it was genuine. I wished I could be more like Wanda, carefree and light-hearted. I was thinking just that when I caught sight of a sparkle of wetness in the corner of her eye. It was there for a split second before she blinked, and then it was gone. God, the war was killing us all. I took her hand and squeezed it. I wanted to be able to protect both her and Sarah from the atrocities in our lives, to be the mother hen for us all, but I couldn't find the strength or the willpower. Instead, I held her hand as we watched the dancers with only the blackness of a scared and skittish city behind them.

At home, I locked the door behind Will and I, ensured the thin film of black wool was drawn over my bedroom window, flicked on the bedside light and laid down on my double bed. Will moved to the dresser where he took off his cap and loosened the buttons of his collar. I watched from my pillow as he doffed his outwear and turned to me wearing loose hunter green shorts that accentuated his arousal.

He knelt beside me on the bed. I reached up to run my hand over his shorn head as he leaned in to kiss me.

His mouth was warm and soft. Running his fingers through my hair he murmured against my cheek, "I've always loved these chestnut curls. Don't ever cut your hair, all right, Emmy? Will you promise?"

"William, dear. It needs the occasional trim. I can't promise that."

"Okay, but don't cut it off. I love it long. I love your braid when you're washing dishes, the ponytail when you're shopping. I want to remember you like this and be able to picture what I'm coming home to."

"I promise." Great. One more thing I wouldn't be able to have control of. While Will was away, I would waste away waiting for him to come home. The urge to defy him and cut my hair there and then was overwhelming, but I bit my tongue and stayed my hand.

Chapter Two

That night the alarms sounded, sending Will bolting from beneath our warm quilts. The building rattled my collection of porcelain music boxes sitting on my dresser. I jumped from the bed to steady them, my trembling hands doing more damage than the onslaught outside. I tried to remind myself that if the walls were shaking, we weren't hit. It was close though and there was no guarantee another bomb wouldn't fall.

A delicate porcelain ballerina crashed to the floor, bringing tears to my eyes. Grandmother Harris would roll in her grave knowing I hadn't protected her antique heirloom.

By the time I reached for the shards of painted porcelain, Will was dressed and searching for his hat.

"Where are you going?" I asked, the breath catching in my throat.

"We'll be sent out now." He paused to read my face. "I'm a pilot, Emmy. It's my job."

I cradled the ballerina against my chest. "I know." I blew him a kiss as he thundered out the door on the heels of the bombers. I knew I'd never see him again. You can ask me how, but I really don't have an answer.

When he was listed as missing in action a week later, I wasn't surprised. I didn't cry as Wanda and Sarah baked me orange cranberry muffins and scones. The amount of tea I drank in those days after the announcement could have floated me away. Drinking and eating gave me something else to think about. I was in limbo once again, waiting for word of his death.

Wanda and Sarah still had their men, although they'd been deployed to the front where the Germans were advancing through France. Will's plane went down as he flew towards Denmark over the North Sea, and he hadn't been heard from since the mission began. I think guilt was most of Wanda and Sarah's motivation in ensuring I ate. I couldn't complain. Their baking was exemplary.

Before we knew it, it was time to let the new girls move into our apartment. Wanda and Sarah secured nice row houses to welcome their men home to. I, on the other hand, had no family in London and no desire to return to Bristol where my mother had her little sewing business. She would want me to return, I was sure of that, but living in her noisy little room near Temple Meade wasn't on my list of things I wanted to do. There wasn't room for the two of us no matter how much we managed to put up with each other. Papa died five years ago of a heart attack. There was no saving him. It had been sudden and thankfully, over quickly. Mother was now too independent to deal with a roommate, even if it was her daughter. I didn't bother to tell her I was currently homeless.

On the day I was to pack and move to a small hotel where I knew I could manage one night, a letter arrived in the mail.

Dear Emeline,

It's been quite some time since we've been able to correspond. However, I'm sure you remember me. I recently heard through the ever-reliable grapevine that your betrothed is no longer with you.

Just this morning I received word that the same terrible fate has taken my husband, Charles. As you know, I live in a small cottage on the edge of a rather large horse farm. I cook for the owner and his staff.

I'd hoped, as we're both alone, that you might consider spending the summer with me. We could be good company for each other and I'm sure it would take some of the unwelcome burden from both of us.

I look forward to hearing your response.

Your loving cousin,
Rose MacDonald.

I hadn't heard from Rose since we were two sixteen year olds in Bristol. She'd married young but did not have any children. Whether that was due to choice or the strange ways of nature, I have no idea and I never asked.

I discussed the letter with Sarah and Wanda who both whole-heartedly agreed that I should leave at once and if it were up to them, they'd go as well. I didn't question who the grapevine was or where it began. No doubt my mother had heard as well, if the news had travelled to Rose already.

Before I could decide not to go, I sent a telegraph to Rose saying that I would be on the train on June the second. She replied that she would be there at five fifteen with the horse and carriage, as she'd run out of money for petrol. Apparently, the cottage wasn't far from the station.

Unsure, I walked alone to the train station, a suitcase full of my two wool sweaters, a pair of trousers and my two day dresses along with a couple of hats, toiletries and my stationary. My dear little music boxes, I had to leave at Sarah's house or find them all broken when I arrived at Pond Hollow, the quaint whistle stop on the route to Bath.

The day was strangely sunny. I say strange because it seemed a grey fog hung over me wherever I went. That I should notice the day being sunny was a revelation. I was doing the right thing. I could feel it in the lightness of my shoulders as I boarded the steam passenger train filled with tots of every size, their eyes filled to the brim with bravely withheld tears as their mothers sent them to relatives in the country to escape the bombing.

I should have felt guilty leaving the city with the children, but I didn't. I wanted to get away from the fear and anxiety pulsing through the streets. If Cousin Rose hadn't written to me, I'm not at all sure I would have survived there.

As the train raced through the green countryside, a thrill of anticipation whipped through me. I felt like sticking my head out the window, letting the full force of the wind rip its icy fingers through my hair, but what kind of example would that have been to the children?

Instead, I paid for a cup of tea and a slice of white frosted cake and sat quietly listening to the consoling of the elder siblings to their young charges. For once, I was thankful to not have children. They'd be safe in the country, but what kind of life was that, away from their parents? Who knew when they'd return home? If ever.

There was a scrabble of feet and arms as the train slowed, approaching Pond Hollow station. Steam erupted from the engine and the chatter of children grew to a fever pitch. I waited until the train ground to a painfully slow stop and most of the children disembarked before I rose from my seat. I adjusted my hat, straightened my skirt and allowed the ticket master to retrieve my suitcase from the storage above my seat. I thanked him graciously, sidled down the aisle and stepped on to the wooden platform.

The children were gathered up and escorted away by their new guardians, leaving me uncomfortably alone on the platform. There was no sign of Rose or any waiting carriage.

"Good God, has she forgotten about me?" I wondered aloud.

"I shouldn't think so, as she sent me." The voice was masculine, deep and smooth. I spun around to find myself overshadowed by the most beautiful man I'd ever seen. For a moment, I was at a total loss for words as I gazed into his rugged face, sharp features softened by a light five-o'clock shadow. I fought the urge to run my hand along his cheek.

Finally, I wet my lips and spoke. "You're here for me?" He didn't seem real.

"Of course." He smiled. "Rose sent me. She managed to twist her ankle on her way to the post box this morning and wondered if I'd be able to meet you and take you to her cottage." He held out his hand. "I'm Ethan Graham."

"Emmy Wood, um…no Rosthorn." I could feel the blush reddening my cheeks as I realised I had no idea which name I should go by. Technically, I wasn't yet married, but I didn't want to disrespect Will's intentions either, especially if he'd died. I decided to give Will's last name.

Belatedly, I shook his hand. In his palm, my hand seemed tiny and frail.

"Emmy Rosthorn. It's a pleasure," he answered, apparently unaware of my embarrassment. He gestured his arm towards an old brown mare, strung to a rickety wagon, blissfully chomping on the grass on the side of the gravel road.

"I'm ready," I said, heaving my suitcase into my arms.

Without speaking, Ethan Graham took the burden from my arms with barely any recognition of its weight and gently set it in the back of the wagon. All the while, I watched his broad back flex beneath his cotton shirt. I blinked my eyes. Why wasn't I thinking of Will? I should have been. I shouldn't have been lusting after some man I'd just met, no matter how attractive he was.

I blew out a deep breath and allowed him to help me into the wagon.

I didn't trust myself to speak on the ride to the cottage. The cool evening air was relaxing and the low golden glow of the sun gave a luscious sheen to everything it touched, including Ethan's dark wavy hair. Worried he'd catch me staring, I shifted slightly to watch the passing forests.

"So, how to do you know Rose?" he asked out of nowhere.

I tried to focus my gaze away from the countryside and back to my driver. He was smiling broadly as if he knew exactly what I was doing.

I cleared my throat. "She's my cousin. As we're both alone right now, we thought we might as well be together. The mood in London after the last bombing is dreadful anyway." I paused. "And you?"

"She cooks at the farm. She lives on the edge of the property."

"And you work there too?"

"You could say that." I though he blushed just a little pink in the cheeks. "I own the farm but I'm out herding cattle and cutting hay most of the day. We're very short on farmhands."

"Ah," I said without much enthusiasm. I wanted to say more but for some reason, I felt like a schoolgirl with a crush around this man.

It wasn't long before he pulled the mare to a stop and nodded towards a small cottage on the side of the road, covered in heaps of vines and roses. From inside the front window, I could see Rose waving frantically. Her excitement was catching and I leaped to my feet.

"Now, hold on just a minute." Ethan leaped from the wagon and jogged over to my side. He held out his hand as any chivalrous knight would and helped me from the wagon. Before releasing my hand, he bent and laid a kiss on my knuckles. Rose completely forgotten, I gazed into his blue eyes; eyes that were eerily the same colour as the twilight sky. Of obvious Welsh descent, his eyes were at odds with his dark colouring. I was intrigued.

As he stood, he pushed back a stray lock of hair from his face and smiled. My heart was thudding in my chest. I hoped he couldn't hear it.

"We'll meet again, I hope," he whispered.

My words stuck in my throat. I tried to clear them and coughed.

"I'm sure we will," I finally managed.

Chapter Three

Inside, the cottage was cosy and cluttered. Bookshelves lined the walls and behind the glassed-in kitchen cupboards were teacups of every size and description. Throws covered the back of the chesterfield and old, yellowed pictures were set and hung wherever there was space.

Rose drew me into an embrace. "I'm so sorry I wasn't there to meet you. It really threw out my day when I wrecked my ankle. It's better now though. See? I'm walking." She turned in a little circle.

"I'm glad you're all right," I said. "Mr. Graham was wonderful to meet the train."

"He's a doll, isn't he? As much as it's up to me to keep the cottage, he helps out quite a bit around here. You know, fixing fences and the like. And he's not bad to look at either. Wait till you see him in uniform."

My heart crashed. Not another one. "He's a soldier?"

"Of course. Aren't they all these days? All the good ones anyway."

"So true." What was it with soldiers and me? Why couldn't I be interested in a nearsighted twig of a man, unfit for military duty?

"Are you alright?" Rose asked.

I knew I'd probably turned pale and was a bit wobbly from missing dinner. "I just need something to eat."

It was Rose's turn to pale. "Oh, my lord! Of course you do. Come with me. I did save you dinner. I just was excited to see you and forgot completely about it. What kind of hostess does that make me?"

"A flattering one, actually," I answered. It was nice to know someone was excited to see me.

* * * *

The next day dawned with a stunning concert of birdsong and bright sunlight. My room at Rose's cottage was entirely too comfortable, and I found I didn't want to leave the warmth of my quilts. It wasn't until I heard a man's voice calling to the cattle in the lower fields to the east of the cottage, that I ventured in my nightdress to the window. I pushed up the sash and leaned outside, the sweet morning breeze bringing the scent of fresh cut hay to my nose. I inhaled deeply. There was nothing like this in London.

In the distance I could see Ethan pitching hay at a few cows gathered around a salt lick. He called each one by name and patted their huge heads as they came up to them.

He taken his shirt off and tucked it into the back of his trousers. Beneath his suspenders, his skin glowed brown from the sun and was shiny with sweat. I'd never wanted to lick a man more in my life. The thought sent my nerves tingling. But it had to remain at that—just a thought. He was a soldier and would no doubt be called away soon. On top of

109

all that, I should have been waiting for Will. I'd yet to be informed of his death.

Just as Ethan looked up and waved to me, I withdrew from the window. I slammed the sash and pulled the curtains. Breathing hard, I flopped back on the bed.

"Breakfast is ready, Emmy," Rose hollered from downstairs.

"Coming," I called back, wishing Ethan hadn't seen me watching him. I wanted to watch him for a while longer without his knowledge. He moved his body with such fluidity, such confidence that he was almost impossible to take my eyes from.

"He's on leave, you know," Rose began. She seemed to be watching me carefully although it may have been my guilt that roused the suspicion.

"Is that so?" I answered warily. I didn't want it to seem that I cared too much.

"He doesn't have any family to visit and so he works the farm. It's his relaxation." I stared out the window at the misty morning fog wondering why a man would choose to be alone on his leave. Most men I knew would find a woman anywhere they could, but there certainly didn't appear to be too many of that sort in Pond Hollow. Most of the women seemed to be taken. Perhaps that was his problem. A night in the brothels of London would have fixed that.

After a quiet breakfast of scrambled eggs and a warm cup of tea to wash it down, I went outside to find Ethan. Neither Rose nor I knew what to say to each other. I expected comfortable support between us regarding our men, however, it didn't happen. We were both too wrapped up in our own lives right then, to properly comfort one another.

That was my take on it anyhow. I think she was as happy to see me out the door after we washed the dishes as I was.

I spent the day walking through the fields and valleys around Pond Hollow. Not entirely sure of my sense of direction, I took Rose's beagle, Hermione, with me. She took her time following me along, snuffing out various rabbit warrens and the odd bird.

The day was warm enough to need a hat for sunshade but cool enough that I wrapped my navy cardigan around my shoulders.

I stopped for lunch in a little bakery on the main street just over the bridge from Rose's cottage. I couldn't resist the scent wafting out into the street. I didn't speak to anyone inside, yet the local crowds watched me closely. Pond Hollow was a small town, full of closely-knit people and the patrons of the bakery were no different. It was obvious to me, that I was the stranger in town and that my actions right then would be my first impression. Where they wondering why I was staying with Rose? No one asked. If they wondered what my intentions were with the bachelor who owned the farm, it didn't come up. I knew I would have to be very careful what I said to Rose. Word would definitely get back to town. I decided to keep my thoughts about Ethan to myself.

It wasn't until after dinner that I noticed a lantern glowing in the loft of the barn. Ethan's broad form cast a dark shadow across the boards of the loft.

Sitting in my room reading a Jane Austin novel, I suddenly had the urge to talk to another human being and my gaze kept being drawn to his fluid shadow in the barn. Rose unfortunately was no conversationalist but that was no matter. I missed having a male in my life. That decided it. It wasn't a sin to want male companionship, was it?

Ethan was pitching hay from the loft of the barn down to the cattle. He was shirtless, his skin smooth and brown from the sun. I watched quietly as he smoothed his dark hair from his forehead. It stuck up momentarily before flopping back down in his eyes. He was the epitome of masculine form.

"Hello," I called up to him. "I'm Emmy Rosthorn."

He grinned at my obvious foolishness. "We've met," he said quietly. I'm sure he thought I didn't notice but his gaze was appreciative as it flicked over my body. I'm sure my face was as red as a cherry, but he gave no indication of noticing. At least he found me somewhat attractive. That was encouraging.

Right that moment as he gazed at me with such intensity, I'd never been lonelier for someone to put his arms around me. It seethed inside me, threatening to pour out all over him.

"Right then. Have a good day," I said, backing away. I wanted him more than anything, but the prospect was also terrifying. I would essentially be having an affair. My mind was in turmoil and completely at odds with the feelings in my body.

"Emmy..."

I turned towards him. "Yes?"

"I'm just on leave." He straightened and leaned on his pitchfork.

"I'm aware of that," I said hesitantly, wondering what he was getting at.

"And you're promised to another."

I crossed my arms over my breasts. "What's that got to do with anything?" I hadn't said anything about my attraction out loud.

"It's why there can't be anything between us." His gaze didn't leave mine.

"Did I ask that of you?"

He bowed his head and kicked at a pile of straw. "All but."

"You seem to know an awful lot about me." I took the opportunity to walk closer to him.

"We're both lonely, Emmy, and you're quite beautiful. I saw you watching me, and I just want you to know where I stand."

"Do you say this to all the girls?" He blushed then and I felt I had some semblance of control over the conversation. I pushed him a bit more. "Did you tell Rose the same thing?"

"Rose is like a sister to me. We practically grew up together and she doesn't have the need inside her that I see in your eyes. And such lovely blue eyes they are, Emmy."

I was close enough now to feel his breath on my face. He smelled of sweet hay, sunshine and sweat. It was a heady mixture. It struck me just how much I missed someone touching me, someone wrapping their arms around me. The feeling was something Will would have understood. I'm more than sure he would have wanted the same thing for himself, if I were lost to him. He would have taken the opportunity, I told myself. And so would I. I reached out to stroke Ethan's upper arm. He didn't move, but his breath hitched in his throat.

"Ethan, what do you think of me? You don't know me. You don't know the man I'm engaged to. Tell me what you're thinking."

He breathed out in a long sigh. "I'm thinking that I'm incredibly drawn to you, and unless I draw up some rules between us, you'll be difficult to resist. We can't do this, Emmy."

I deliberately unbuttoned the collar of my white blouse, displaying my cleavage to his eager gaze. He couldn't seem to lift his face to meet mine. I bit my lip, knowing I had him.

"Yes, we can, Ethan. We will."

The enormity of the circumstance was increasingly apparent from the changes beneath his trousers. I kept myself from cupping him, although it was what I wanted more than anything. It would have solidified my intentions. Instead, he made the move.

His arm snaked around my waist. I knew it was an instinctive gesture because his gaze was locked with mine and didn't seem to register the contact. It surprised him when I moved up against his broad chest, allowing his arms to tighten around me.

His pulse beat rapidly under my palm, his breath whispering sweetly over my lips. The kiss was just out of reach but I didn't want to push him too far. It had to be his move. I couldn't be labelled a tramp in such a small town. If he turned on me and blabbed, I'd have to go back home. That was something I wasn't quite ready for. It had taken all my energy just to leave London.

I wet my lips, waiting impatiently. As I tilted my head and moved a touch closer, he made his move. Unfortunately, it wasn't the one I was hoping for. He released his arms and took a step back.

"You're taken, Emmy. I can't do that to the man who holds you in his heart."

"He's dead, Ethan," I said, pushing disappointment out of my expression. Even as the words came out of my mouth, I knew it to be true. Up until that moment, I truly hadn't felt it. I hadn't allowed myself to think about it, but yes, I just needed the confirmation from the RAF. William was dead to me.

As he considered my words, my eyes brimmed with tears. It was the first I'd considered that the only thing I missed about William were his warm arms around my body. I was torn between feeling like a traitor and feeling like a needed woman.

"How can you be sure?" he whispered, once again drawing me close. I pressed my face into his chest.

"I can't explain, but he's not coming back for me, and I don't want to be alone right now."

Ethan's chest expanded in a deep sigh. His heavy hand cradled my head. "Ah, Emmy. I do want you. Who wouldn't? But, you don't need me. You're a strong woman."

"You don't know me well enough to say that." I nuzzled his neck, my challenges growing bolder.

"I know you left everything behind to be here with Rose. I know you're not a basket case after losing your future husband. You're more woman than you think."

I tried to keep from trembling in his arms. He was right. Perhaps I didn't need him quite as badly as I first thought, but I certainly wanted him. Making the final decision, I slipped my fingers beneath the waistband of his trousers.

I smiled when his breath choked in his throat.

"You're a wicked woman, Ms. Woods," he answered, deliberately using my maiden name.

"Then, be wicked *with* me Mr. Graham."

"Anything we do won't be done lightly in my mind. You're beautiful, Emmeline and I can see by your expressions how bright you are. I know you are lonely, and I won't say I'm not. In that way, we're perfect for each other but I want you to know that emotion comes with what we're thinking. It cannot be done without emotion. I would brand you."

His mouth came down on mine before I had time to take a breath. He pulled me hard against his chest as his hand snaked inside my blouse. He cupped my breast as I raced to rid myself of my clothing. All the while, his lips sought my jaw, the tender skin of my neck and down to my collar bone.

Each kiss felt like a searing hot burn. I arched back as he reached to take my nipple in his mouth. The electricity that followed as he flicked the nipple with the tip of his tongue buckled my legs.

How I'd gone from watching him from my window to bowing under his powerful kiss was almost unimaginable, had I not been experiencing it myself.

Releasing my breast, he held my weight with one hand while trailing his fingers down my neck. He reached under my skirt, hiking it up. As his mouth once again took over mine and our tongues slid languidly against one another, pulling a moan from deep in side me. Then, as a wave of want washed over me, I wrapped my leg around his thigh. At the same moment, he cupped me between my legs, pushing his fingers into the soft folds and rubbing them tortuously against my clitoris.

I knew I was wet and wondered if he felt it as well. I ground against his experienced hand, hoping he would acknowledge the encouragement to take things further. I was well past worrying about what anyone would think of the situation, including myself.

For a moment, I pulled away, reaching for the button at the top of his trousers. His erection was solid, hot against my thigh and enticingly large. I wanted to feel it in my hands, to feel his warmth and his eagerness. Sliding my hand down the inside of his pants brought out his breath in quick, shallow pants. It was all the encouragement I needed.

Just as my fingers touched the smooth skin of his shaft, it jerked to attention. He pushed his trousers down to his thigh and his erection sprang free, reaching eagerly towards his belly. I wrapped my hands around his shaft and stroked up to the silky tip, surprised that my fingers barely met as they encircled his girth. As I moved to stroke him faster Rose called from the cottage.

"Emmy? Emmy, where are you?"

"Oh, good Lord," I muttered, dropping my head.

Ethan laid his chin on the top of my head. "You'd better go see what she wants."

I inhaled deeply and withdrew my hand. "This isn't over."

"I sure hope not." He bowed his head to me as I picked up my skirt so I wouldn't trip and jogged towards the cottage.

Chapter Four

By the time I reached Rose, whose face was flushed with yelling, the throbbing deep in my core had subsided. As far as I knew, there was no outward sign of what I'd been up to in the barn.

"I've been looking all over for you," Rose complained. For the first time, her voice grated on my ears. My forehead furrowed in annoyance.

"I was just exploring," I answered with as much cheeriness as I could muster.

She wiped at her forehead. "It's just so easy to get lost in the fields, especially at night. I feel responsible for you. I thought maybe you were lost."

I followed her into the cottage. "I'll be sure to let you know where I'm headed from now on."

Rose collapsed into an armchair where she picked up a worn novel.

"What are you reading?" I asked without much true interest.

She held up the book. "Rebecca DeMourney. She's wonderful, really."

Wondering how I could possibly entertain myself when Ethan wasn't around, I asked, "Could I borrow it when you're finished?"

"Of course." She immersed herself in her book, leaving me to my own devices. God, what had I gotten myself into? I didn't want to be in London, I didn't want to be in Bristol and now, I didn't really want to be in Pond Hollow. Ethan was the only saving grace about the place but he was taking more work than I thought. I wandered through the cottage, my hands behind my back, with no destination. Trying to escape the unease, I retreated, alone, to my room upstairs.

Although it was still dark outside and I should have been asleep, I couldn't. I was still aching for release. About to solve the problem myself, I jumped when I heard my name called from outside my window. I smoothed my skirt and placed my hands on the sill.

"Ethan? Is that you?" I called.

"Em, I brought you a horse. Let's take a ride." His voice was full of a confidence I hadn't heard from him before. I squinted through the darkness to see the shadow of two horses below in the garden, one with a rider. Still, I hesitated.

"Tell Rose you're coming, if it would make you feel better. I promise to be good," he urged.

I smiled down at him, hoping he could see my face. "Not too good, though. Right?" I teased.

"Only as good as you want me to be, but you can tell Rose I've come to take you for a ride into town. You're a grown woman. She won't be put out by it."

I nodded and reached for my cardigan.

Seeing Ethan again, had a strangely calming effect on my tense body. It was as if I knew instinctively that my body was his for the taking and it had decided to wait patiently.

Rose didn't have a problem with Ethan taking me out. She adored him and held him in the highest respect both as a man and as her employer. I think she was a little infatuated with him herself. She told me I was perfectly safe in his company. How little she knew. My heart was anything but safe in his hands.

Once he'd helped me mount the mare, we led the horses down the drive and along the main road.

"I hope you don't mind my coming for you," he began.

"Of course not."

He glanced at me. "You weren't in bed?"

"Almost, but I wasn't undressed yet." I thought that made him blush a little but I couldn't see his face well enough in the dark.

"I enjoy being with you, Em. I feel as if I've always known you," he said quietly.

I cleared my throat, a little unsure of how to respond. "I feel that way too, Ethan," I said honestly. "I'm really glad you're the one who met me at the station. This stay with Rose could have been the worst thing for my life right now, if you hadn't been here."

Ethan led the horses to a creek just north of town. There, he tied the horses loosely to a tree so they could drink. He helped me down and swung me into his arms. This time, his kiss was gentle. Instead of making me throb, it melted my insides. He wrapped his arms around my back and slowly drew me closer to him. I complied, closed my eyes and allowed my body to assume a languid state so that it moulded into his solid curves.

His erection was hard on my thigh, yet he made no move to alleviate any discomfort he must have been feeling. All of his focus seemed to be on me.

When he broke the kiss and my eyes flickered open, he was watching me, his eyelids heavy and with a smile on his lips.

"That was nice," I whispered. "More than nice."

"I'm glad. I just wanted you to know that I'm not the kind of man who will take any woman he can have. And you're not any woman."

My heart fluttered just a bit. My lips parted yet no words formed in my mind.

"I'm glad you came here, Em. I like being with you, and I'll be here for anything you need. If that's a man in your bed, I'm ready."

"There's nowhere else I'd rather be right now than with you," I told him sincerely.

We rode back to the cottage in silence. It was almost as if he were apologising for his ardour in the barn, but I didn't think that was it. He wasn't the kind of man to apologise for what he was feeling. Could it be he simply wanted me to know that he was there for me, in all respects? I wondered how long my heart could take being spoiled by Ethan Graham.

* * * *

The following night was uncommonly humid, threatening a storm. I hadn't seen Ethan since our ride the night before. Despite our conversation, it was as if he was hiding from me. I wouldn't have blamed him. What kind of woman was I, who would sleep with an RAF pilot when my own was still missing? I'm sure that's what was going through his head. I know, because it was going through mine. When I was with Ethan, there was nothing in the world that was important. My thoughts and feelings revolved around him. Then, later, when I was alone, all my guilt and insecurities would surface once again.

I went down to the river, which wound its way alongside the cottage and behind the farm. Lined with willow trees and soft mosses, it was a wondrous place. I'd been only once before on one of my walks with Hermione. Fairies could have been living there, among the flowing branches, and I wouldn't have been surprised.

I smoothed my skirt under my bottom and sat in the moss to watch the river meander through the woods. The scent was heavenly, all earth and cleanliness. I breathed it in as deeply as I could.

My gaze lingered on the far bank. When a man surfaced from beneath the soft, rippling of the water, my eyes widened. He was brown from the sun right down to his white buttocks that shone with perfection in the blue twilight. He reached up to run his fingers through his wet hair and the muscles in his back that tapered down to his lean waist flexed and moved with a grace I'd never seen.

When his profile came into view, it confirmed what I already knew. I was watching Ethan wash the dirt from his body after a day of working the farm. As he climbed the opposite bank, I couldn't tear my gaze from the dark mass hanging heavy between his legs. It came into view with every step before disappearing again. When he turned fully, completely nude in the glimmering, ethereal light, he could have been otherworldly himself, a being sent from the stars to please my eyes. His chest was smooth but a dark trail of hair spread from his navel deep into his groin where it nested his cock. It twitched and I looked up, the spell broken.

By the time I realised he was watching me, it was too late. I'd been staring for quite some time. Determined not to look a fool, I inhaled deeply, met his gaze and gave him a coy smile. His cheeks reddened, giving me confidence.

"See something you like?" he asked, his gaze dark. Even though he was perhaps fifty feet from me, each detail of his speech, his body and his expression was vividly detailed.

I stood, dusting off my behind. "I see something I want, but there's a river between us," I said with as much sensuality as I could manage in my needy state. I was essentially throbbing, inside and out. Having him inside me was the only thing that would sate the need.

He remained quiet for a moment, then, dropped the shirt he'd picked up and dove back into the water. Holding his breath as his lithe body slid just below the surface, he seemed a nymph god, completely at home in his underwater world. If I'd had a camera, it would have been the perfect picture.

When he emerged and took a deep, cleansing breath, a smile lit his face. "See, nothing to it. Can't let a river come between us, can we?"

So, he'd changed his mind about our relationship? Was that what he was telling me? A shiver rippled through my body. He climbed from the water, naked and shining. Taking hold of my shoulders, Ethan leaned closer. He kissed me hard, with no hesitation, no tentative probing, as I would have expected of our first time together. His body, hard and wet, pressed against mine and I momentarily wondered how I would explain wet clothing to Rose if she weren't yet asleep when I returned home. No matter. I didn't intend on returning to the cottage any time soon.

Ethan was hard and insistent. He laid me back on the ground, looming over me with lust rippling over him.

The sensation of soft moss tickling my back forced me to writhe, creating a bed for my body. The writhing motion of my hips added to his ardour. I was a petite woman but my curves were lush and feminine. He knew I was watching him, but he couldn't take his eyes off my skin. Slowly, he brushed aside my blouse, revealing my pert, soft breasts. His fingers trailed languidly around the outer curves eliciting a shiver from deep within me. He glanced at my face. I closed my eyes, my lips slightly parted and from the heat, I knew my cheeks were flushed.

If he slipped his hand beneath the waistband of my skirt, he'd find me ready for him. It seemed I was always ready for him, no matter the time of day or circumstances. He roused in me, sensations I'd never before experienced.

"I don't just want the sex, Em. I want to make you mine," he breathed as he focused his attention on my curves. He leaned closer and nuzzled my neck, nipping at my earlobe. Where his palm rested on my breast, he felt my long inhalation.

I couldn't answer him just then. I had no idea what to say, so I left it at that. He'd made it clear that any intimacy between us wouldn't be without emotion on his part, however, I didn't know what it would be for me.

I reached up and took hold of his biceps as he moved overtop of me. He was achingly hard as I raked my hands down his back. He straightened for a brief moment to take me in. Immediately, my hands went for his chest where they played with his dusting of hair. He lowered his body so that my warmth heated his skin and my breasts cushioned his chest. Rubbing himself against my thigh in gentle circles, he let out a gasp when I reached down to cup him in my palm. His balls were heavy and big. I moved to use both hands so that I could knead him gently. He inhaled deeply when I slowly tugged before reaching for his waist.

Ethan took my head in his hands and kissed me deeply.

"You taste of warmth, of life and…cinnamon," he said.

I laughed. "Cinnamon buns for breakfast," I whispered.

I wrapped my full lips around his tongue and he allowed me to suck and pull as he pressed his shaft against my damp folds. I gasped as his cock touched my tingling skin and within seconds he was buried to the hilt within me. He stretched me, filled me until I could no longer speak. A thousand sensations broke over me before he could even begin his own rhythm. The wetness of his skin smelled of rain, his cold body warming quickly over mine, the rapid breathing close to my ear and the explosion of light in front of my eyes, as my nipples met his chest, blended with the night sounds of the river and the incoming clouds.

From his expression, I knew this was going to be over faster than he'd anticipated. He withdrew but when I whimpered in protest against his ear, he repositioned himself and thrust hard. There was nothing I wanted more and as I forced myself to relax in order to accept all of him, he slowly slid deeper.

He seemed to hit all the right spots and as he moved within me, I convulsed against him, throwing my legs around his lean waist. Before my closed eyes, pinpricks of light danced in circles. I could have lain there all night, just like that, without him even moving, but there was more to come.

Panting now, he reverted to an instinctual rhythm. This was so much different than any night I'd spent with Will. Then, it had been for comfort, for companionship. This time, as I clenched my muscles tightly around his shaft, it was for pure pleasure. I was his in that moment, and I'd fight to remember it for the rest of my life.

With the pressure inside me building, he thrust his hands beneath my bottom, angling me so that he entered deeply. I moaned despite the fact that I was pinned under most of his body weight. I tossed my head as he bent to nip my collarbone. His thrusts were insistent, as if he had been waiting a lifetime for this moment. All his pent up emotions raged through him and into me. I lifted my knees. He grasped behind them and groaned as he continued to sate his long pent-up lust.

The deeper penetration and the new position sent waves of electricity shooting through my system. I arched beneath him, my body no longer under my control. Inside, I was a throbbing entity, milking him for what I needed. I came hard, my muscles tight as my body begged him to come with me. I knew my fingernails were biting his shoulders but I couldn't have done a thing to stop.

He rode me over the crest and as he gazed into my eyes, I felt the beautiful floating sensation as I came back to earth.

He straightened then and I bit my lip when he swelled inside me, knowing the end was near. Stretching so that his chest was above my face, he almost lost control when I took his nipple into my mouth. That was it. He thrust hard as if not wanting to be without the tight warmth holding him inside me. Then, without warning, every muscle in his body clenched, his shaft pulsed with release and he emptied inside me.

I pulled him down on top of me before he could give any thought to his weight. I bore all of him, keeping my legs wrapped tightly around him and God, did I love him on top of me.

For a moment he stayed that way until he noticed my breathing becoming shallow. It didn't bother me in the slightest but he slid to my side, pulling me against him. My eyes were closed now and he laid a kiss on one eyelid bringing a peaceful smile to my face.

* * * *

Still shuddering with lust and serenity, the cold rain landed in my eye. For a moment, I thought it must be drops from his hair, but he was relaxed, his head beside mine, our bodies still joined.

The first bolt of lightning blinded me and I saw spinning circles of light until I rubbed at my eyes. The subsequent thunder had Ethan pulling from me and sitting upright. I watched him as he gazed at the sky, a worried expression on his face.

"Do you think he's angry?" he asked.

"Who?" I whispered, thinking he might mean William, as the rain cooled my now exposed belly.

"The man upstairs." He rubbed at his forehead.

That surprised me. "I didn't know you were religious," I said.

"Only sometimes." He smiled at me, and I realised how serious he took our situation. He honestly didn't want me to be cheating on Will, nor did he want to disgrace Will's memory by screwing his fiancée so soon after his death.

I rubbed the arm he was leaning on, hoping to offer some comfort. If he thought what we'd done was wrong, I wasn't sure I could live with the thought that I'd seduced him, no matter how bad I'd wanted it.

"Like right now?" I asked.

He didn't answer me. "We'd better get inside."

Another bolt of lightning tore across the now-black sky, leaving tinges of red and purple in its wake. The thunder seemed to shake the trees. I grabbed my panties and straightened the rest of my clothes.

"Good idea," I said, now more fearful than just a moment earlier. The dark sky seemed to be rolling and the rain was pelting.

"We'll get to the barn," he suggested. "It's closer."

He stood and reached down his hand to help me up. I slipped on my panties, hastily grabbing for my other clothes. Cradling them against my breast, I ran hand in hand with Ethan towards the dark shadow of the barn.

Inside the barn, it was as dark as my bedroom in London with the blackout curtains drawn. Here, they were required as well, only the citizens of Pond Hollow were usually tucked in bed before they needed any electric lights. Well, Rose was anyway. I suppose I can't speak for the other residents.

As Ethan moved around the barn, seeming to know what he was looking for, I stood still, afraid of running into something or tripping over some farm implement. The soft movement of the few calves, rustling straw as they slept in their stalls, gave a comforting sound to a building that otherwise would have been full of eerie creaks and cold drafts. It was anything but cold, which was good because we were both dripping wet. Dying of pneumonia wasn't on my list of to-do items.

Ethan returned to me, skimming his strong hand over my shoulder before escorting me to a stack of hay at the north end of the barn. Here, he layered the blankets he'd collected. Together, we snuggled deep inside and simply lay in each other's arms. I couldn't remember ever feeling this way with Will. He had been practical where Ethan was obviously impulsive and romantic. But no, I didn't want to think of Will. He was dead.

"I want to marry you, Emmy," he said out of the darkness.

I froze and held my breath. "No, you don't." *Not again*, I thought with a sense of resignation.

His arms tightened their hold on me. "I know we barely know each other, but don't you hear stories about people knowing when it's right?" I moved to speak but he shushed me. "Emmy. I know you're grieving, but there is time for us."

I took a deep breath. "And when you get called into service again? When your leave is over? What happens to me then? I'm not sure I can handle it again, Ethan."

"We can deal with that when the time comes," he said impulsively.

I turned towards him, my lips brushing his jaw line. "Ethan, listen to me. I don't want to be a waiting wife. I didn't want it before Will left and I don't want it now. I didn't know you were a pilot when I first met you. You drew me in under false pretences."

He laughed, his whole body shaking around me. "I did nothing of the sort. I believe it was you who seduced me."

"All right," I said on a sigh. "You're right. I did. I'd missed that sort of comfort so much. Can you see that? I won't apologise. I'd do it all over again in an instant."

"I don't expect you to," he said with a wistful tone in his voice. "It's just that I've waited so long to find the right woman for me. I've never married just because a local girl took a fancy to me, but somehow, it just feels right with you. I've only known you for a few days, but..." He didn't finish.

I couldn't tell him I felt the same. The ghost of William was too nearby as was the prospect of my own self being lost once again. Being married, waiting for a fighter pilot, it was all so depressing, so much like living under a wet blanket. I couldn't let it start again.

"I want you Ethan. But I don't want to be married. I've been there and it nearly destroyed me." His smile disappeared. "I'll be here for you if you need me when you return. I'll be here for this, but not as a wife." I turned in his arms towards him. "And I can't guarantee there won't be others."

The words hurt as soon as they came out. The tension in his muscles and his silence told me I'd wounded him, but the sting in my throat and the clutch of my chest was completely unexpected. The fact was, I didn't want others. I wanted him, here, time and time again. But, I didn't want him holding out for me. I was afraid it would be just as tortuous for him as it would be for me. Was that supposed to be part of life? The torture? I hoped not, but it was starting to seem inescapable. What did I know? All I knew was that I didn't want him missing out on his life because he was worried about me.

"Say something, Ethan."

He cleared his throat. "I'm sorry. I wasn't expecting that. This is a small town. I assumed your want of me indicated the possibility of a prolonged relationship."

Why so formal? I wondered, but I didn't say that out loud. It felt like he was pulling away.

I'm not certain when we fell asleep. Despite our disheartening discussion, we made love another time before settling into the hay to sleep in each others arms, exhausted and empty.

In the morning, when I peeked in the windows of the cottage before entering, Rose was nowhere to be found. I climbed the rickety stairs of the quiet cottage, thinking to change my clothes, find a sunhat and take the dog for a walk. Rose's beagle, Hermione, followed me up the stairs, somehow sensing my intentions. Her light pants accompanied me into my adopted room where my attention was immediately drawn to the bed.

Sitting alone on the thick quilt was a rumpled envelope, neatly rimmed in black. My breath caught in my throat, just as the old cliché describes, and it literally took a moment for my involuntary functions to kick in. My fingers shaking, I picked up the envelope. I don't know why I was shaking, because the content of the envelope was quite obvious. But, for some reason, I couldn't open it in that room. Will wasn't a part of Pond Hollow. Instead, I walked out to the river, where I'd spent the evening before. There was something healing about the river. Even without Ethan's presence, it felt right to sit there on the moss and read of Will's passing.

...battle with the Luftwafte over the north sea...has now been confirmed deceased. His aircraft, a heavy Whitley bomber, was found by a patrolling U-boat, still containing the bodies of Lieutenant William Rosthorn and his wingman...not able to eject...

It went on for several paragraphs, but only a few sentences struck me. A strange trickle of relief began at the top of my head and ran down through my body. It was confirmed. William was dead. So, now what did that mean? Truly, it changed nothing, only that I knew I no longer was expected to wait for him. But it wasn't the relief I expected. For the first time, I recognised the ache in my chest as being the place Will had once occupied. Since he'd left, I'd been telling myself I didn't love him, that I shouldn't have to deprive myself of male company just because he left on a mission, but reading that letter cleared up all my confusions. I had loved him in a way, but I loved Ethan, too and quite possibly, with more intensity, more passion. After such a short time, I knew I wouldn't be able to recover from Ethan's death, should it occur. I had to do something to keep him from flying.

I thought the answer might come to me if I went to see Ethan. However, seeing him left me just as confused as before. I'd intended to talk with him, urge him to leave the

RAF, to run, go AWOL. I knew deep inside, it wasn't a possibility, but I felt I had to try. Anyway, I was distracted.

Chapter Five

I walked into the barn with Hermione on my heels. The scent of clean leather was pervasive. I think I'll always associate leather with Ethan, just because of that moment. Ethan was scrubbing down the tack for the horses, no doubt intending to take his own out for a ride. I stopped in the doorway to watch him. The smooth planes of his back glistened with sweat. The ridges of his farm-grown muscles flexed as he stretched his arm out over the saddle with a damp cloth in his hand. He raked his free hand through his hair, bringing on the throb between my legs that seemed now to always accompany his presence.

I watched him move effortlessly to sling the saddle up over the side of the stall where he left it to dry. I jumped when he spoke.

"I've been called to London," he said without looking in my direction. I didn't think I'd made any noise but he obviously knew I was there.

At his words, I gripped the doorframe to support myself. *Not another one*, I thought. *I'm too late*. The war would kill them all, given the chance.

"You won't come with me?" He snuck a peek over his bare shoulder. If he was hoping to catch my reaction, I'm sure I disappointed him. I'd been expecting this and stilled my expression.

"No," I said simply. Inside, I screamed, *Yes! Yes, Ethan, take me with you!*

He nodded in acceptance. "Do you love me, Em?"

"No," I lied. The truth was that I didn't know right then what I should say. Some days I wouldn't have known love if it walked up and introduced itself, but now? I just knew I wanted him in my life, forever. I changed the subject. "The letter came today. Will is dead. Shot down over the North Sea."

He turned to look at me. "I thought as much."

Anger flashed through me as fast as a burning forest. How dare he remain so impassive? "You did not! You couldn't possibly have known. Whatever guilt you're feeling, you just can't pass if off like that."

I have no idea why I was so mad, but all the anger I'd been feeling about Will leaving me suddenly burst out all over Ethan. It wasn't fair to him, but he understood.

As soon as my face flushed with anger he moved towards me. By the end of my little tirade, I was in his arms. He held me tight as if I might hurt him or myself if he let me go. My hot tears dried on his warm chest. I didn't want to move. If I could have chosen one spot to stay for the rest of my life, it would have been in the arms of this pilot. I clung to him and he let me. His solid body became my rock, my anchor and my buoy.

When I'd calmed, Ethan gently pulled me into the straw where we'd made our bed the night before. His strong hand pushed the mussed hair from my face at the same moment as he leaned in to kiss me.

He'd never kissed me like that before. It was tender, claiming and loving all at once.

"You love me, don't you?" I whispered, without opening my eyes.

He hesitated. "I do, Em. I want you to come with me to London. I'll be back. I'm not your William."

"He was never mine." I opened my eyes and touched Ethan's rough cheek. He was warm and familiar and his essence sparked through me. God, how was I going to survive this? "I think I must have known that all along. It wasn't my job to wait for him. He was never for me. His death didn't crush me, whereas yours…"

He silenced me with his mouth. As he did, he hiked up my skirt and discarded my panties.

The thought that I aroused him to this extent slicked my inner thighs with moist heat.

When rid of his clothing, I couldn't help but gasp as Ethan's thick shaft rose up eagerly towards my waiting hands. Beneath, his testicles hung heavy and swollen. I reached out to grasp him and when I did, he sucked in his breath at my light touch.

Rearing over me, he forced me to lie back. I gasped as he pressed his arousal against my folds. He held my gaze as he pressed into me, seeming to be gauging my reaction.

In the same moment, Ethan groaned, and he stretched me. The healing pressure was intense and I cried out beneath him. He smothered my mouth with his, taking in my cries of pleasure, distracting me as he pushed deeper. The sensation of fullness as he pressed to the hilt, enveloped me with warmth and I ached to take him deeper.

He began to move then. I savoured the intense friction and the weight of his body on mine. I closed my eyes. It felt as if every nerve ending in my body was alive. If he touched my cheek, my breast, my hip, my entire body reacted.

I clung to his shoulders as he wrapped his hand beneath my bottom. The new angle was thrilling. I gasped and tensed with passion. Stars danced in front of my closed eyes and when my body arched up in release, those stars burst and convulsions rippled through me from the inside out.

Within moments, I felt Ethan swell inside me. He groaned and drove into me, holding his position as I stroked the ridges of muscles on his back. I could feel the quick pulses and the rushing warmth as he emptied into me. As his breathing calmed, Ethan withdrew and settled beside me on his back. He drew me against him as I pulled a woollen blanket over the top of our sated bodies.

Taking my hand in his, he grazed my knuckles with his soft mouth, eliciting a shudder from me.

"I won't leave you, Em. I'll always come back for you," he moaned.

He held me tight, as if to assure me that it wasn't just the act he wanted. It was the closeness he needed. And I wanted him there.

* * * *

I packed in the morning and caught the train from Pond Hollow to London with Ethan. We stayed the night in a small, dingy hotel, near the train station, making the most of our last hours together. It wasn't much, but it was everything.

I knew then that waiting for Ethan wouldn't be the hardship it seemed to be with William. I was honoured to wait for him. His short, handwritten letters that came in the mail while he was away thrilled me. When I worried about his death, it wasn't me and my loneliness I was concerned about, it was Ethan. And yes, if something had happened to him, I would have been ruined, devastated, by what I'd lost.

By the grace of God, Ethan was returned to me time and time again until the end of the war. Now, when his face lights up as he holds his cooing son in the evenings, I know he'll be with me always. I have loved him from the day we first met.

DOUBLE TIME

SL Majors

Dedication

For Bev… This one really is all yours!

Chapter One

"Absolutely not." Captain Trent Williams's fingers formed a death-grip around the pint of beer on the table in front of him. Jaynie, his younger sister's best friend, could beg and cajole all night long. But he wasn't budging. "I am not fucking a woman I've never met. No matter how long I've been in the desert." Or how horny he was. He had morals and scruples to go along with his hard dick.

"It's only for two days," Jaynie shouted above the noise.

Clayton, his mate since university, hid his laugh by taking a deep swig from the amber liquid in his mug. What the hell was a best friend for, anyway, if not to laugh his ass off when his mate was faced with female disaster?

It was no accident that she'd invited him and Clayton to a public place that served up loud, throbbing music, cocktail waitresses in short, short skirts, and lots and lots of beer. Get him liquored up, that would be Jaynie's plan, and then move in for the kill.

She batted her baby blues hopefully. "Please, Trent? It's for a good cause. Promise."

"It's always for a good cause. Last time it was posing for a calendar with a puppy."

"And we raised a mint for the dog shelter."

Unfortunately for her and this week's charity, he was wiser than he'd been last time he was home. And he'd made sure not to drink more than a pint.

"Sorry, love. You'll have to find some other bloke."

"Blokes."

"I beg your pardon?"

"Blokes." She repeated. "The lady in question specifically requested you..." Jaynie had the good grace to flush with embarrassment before glancing at the table. "And Clayton."

Trent looked at his comrade.

"Wait. Both of us?" Clayton asked.

"She doesn't just want me? She wants...?" Trent trailed off, snapping his mouth shut. Jaynie was a harebrained mastermind, but this? She might as well have dropped an IED in the middle of the room.

"Yes. And she's willing to pay for it. Uh, for you. Willing to pay for both of you. Handsomely, I might add." She smiled sunnily, her embarrassment apparently forgotten. "Did I mention it's for a good cause?"

"Jesus, Jaynie," Clayton said. Beer sloshed over the rim of his glass. "Trent's right. You're out of your mind."

"Not so funny now, is it, mate?"

"What kind of woman pays for sex with a stranger?" Clayton asked.

"Not *a* stranger," she corrected. "Two of them. Actually, you both have quite the reputation in town, so it's not as if you're an unknown. Actually, I wish I'd thought of it myself. I'd have bought you in a heartbeat."

Clayton choked on a drink of beer. Trent smacked him on the back.

142

"It was the calendar," Jaynie said, going on as if neither had spoken. "Mr. July." She nodded to Trent. "Hot enough to sizzle for summer. And Mr. December." She grinned at Clayton. "Cool as ice. In fact..." She reached into her handbag and pulled out a cheque book. She uncapped a ballpoint pen, then started to scrawl her signature on the bottom line.

Trent's blood heated to a slow boil. "We are not sleeping with you, Jaynie."

"Then...?"

"Or the mystery woman," he added.

She pouted. "Ten thousand pounds."

"Ten thousand..." Clayton trailed off.

"And it's all or nothing. She gets both of you, or she wants neither. Think about it." She dropped her pen and curled her hand around Trent's wrist. "No one will ever know."

"Not like the damn calendar," Clayton grumbled.

"Ten thousand quid to benefit John MacDougal's family."

"Fuck." John MacDougal's family. He'd served in the Middle East with John. Fine man. Fine soldier. With three-year-old twins. Fuck. Trent took a long drink from his beer. "That's low, Jaynie, even for you."

"I didn't make the offer," she said, softly. The teasing was gone. Nothing but the weight of a fallen comrade shrouded the table. Even the music seemed to recede.

They all knew John and Susan. Jaynie had gone to school with the couple. He and Clayton knew John from the Army. Trent remembered that the man had carried a picture of the twin girls and his wife in his pocket, tucked inside a small Bible. *Fuck.*

"What does she want us to do?"

At Clayton's question, Trent raised a brow.

"She's willing to send a car for you on Friday, around tea time. You'll be returned on Sunday, most likely in the afternoon, if that suits you. You could probably negotiate a longer stay if needed." She smiled sweetly, innocently. She was neither, Trent knew.

"That wasn't my question," Clayton said.

"Oh, the usual, I suppose." She waved a hand dismissively. "Whatever it is that two men do when they get a sexy woman in bed."

"Sexy?" Clayton asked.

Trent shouldn't have clapped Clayton on the back. He should have boxed the man's ears. The idea was preposterous. Outrageous.

"Sexy," Jaynie repeated.

"So why is she paying for a fuck?" Trent asked.

"You're being crude, Captain."

"Answer Clayton's question, Jaynie."

"I didn't ask. I took the money and ran."

Very carefully, he enunciated each word. "You took the money?"

"Oh. Uhm. Well…"

He let her dangle from the noose of her own words.

"I knew you wouldn't say no, not when you knew it was for Susan and the wee babies." This time, she appealed to Clayton. Smart woman. "You like don't have to touch each other. Just her. I think."

"What the hell?" Trent demanded.

She ignored him and continued to look at Clayton. "You could even take turns. One of you in her bedroom at a time. Wear a condom if you want."

"Jaynie," Trent warned.

"Ten thousand quid," she said again. "Not for you, for the MacDougals."

"Susan needs it," Clayton reminded Trent. "And we always said we'd do what we needed to in order to help out."

He looked from Clayton to Jaynie, and then back again. They had both lost their collective minds. The calendar was beginning to look as if it had been one of her better ideas.

"She's John's widow, Clayton." Jaynie stroked the back of Clayton's hand and ignored Trent. "No commitments or obligations. You'll be making the generous donor happy as well as helping Susan and the children."

Trent brought his fist down on the table. All three beer mugs jumped. "Forget it."

"I'm in," Clayton said.

Trent blinked. "You're what?"

"It's for a good cause, mate. Queen and country and all that."

Jaynie leaned over and kissed Clayton's cheek, leaving a little streak of pink lipstick on his freshly shaven cheek. The man preened like a freaking peacock.

They were talking about fucking a woman they'd never met.

Grinning like an idiot, Clayton said, "Any port in a storm, hey, Trent?"

They were soldiers, for chrissake, not sailors. "We are not doing this."

"I am," Clayton said softly. "Ten thousand quid. Hell, I've fucked for a lot less noble causes than this one."

Jaynie turned to look at Trent. "You can't say no."

"The hell I can't."

"But you won't," said Clayton, suddenly serious, suddenly assertive.

Trent scowled. When in the name of all things holy had his buddy decided this was a good idea, and for him, too?

"We've talked about sharing a woman before."

Which was probably too much information in front of Jaynie, but she just kept on smiling. Well, why wouldn't she. She was close to getting what she wanted. Ten thousand quid to help a soldier's wife.

Put that way, it didn't seem so unpalatable.

"Do the right thing, Trent." Clayton raised a pint of beer in mock salute. "Now, Jaynie, tell me something about our mystery lady, besides the fact she's dripping money?"

"She wants you both in uniform. Well, at least to start with, I imagine."

"Do we know who she is?"

"She's a bit younger than you are. Micah Collins."

Clayton shook his head, but Trent said, "I've heard of her."

"Then you know you'd happily pay to sleep with *her*." Jaynie reached over and patted his cheek.

Trent had only two questions, what in the hell was happening here? And why the hell wasn't he stopping it?

* * * *

Micah Collins dragged her fingers through her hair, dislodging a pin. The metal pinged as it hit the ceramic tiled kitchen floor.

She was completely out of her mind.

What *had* she been thinking when she'd written that cheque? Oh yes, that she could do a good thing by making a significant donation to the military fundraiser. She was supporting Crown and country.

Oh hell.

Who was she trying to fool?

She'd wanted to take care of her pesky problem. For the love of God, how many twenty-five year old virgins were there in Britain?

So how did she decide to solve the problem of her virginity?

By buying two men. And not just any two men. Captains Trent Williams and Clayton Blackwell. Two of the county's bravest and sexiest soldiers.

They had dominated her dreams since girlhood. Several years ahead of her in school, they'd been the older boys she and her friends had whispered about on the phone.

She'd wanted to be kissed and held and romanced.

They'd never even known she was alive.

Then they'd grown up and gone away to university. The next time she'd seen them, they'd been in uniform.

Oh, Lord.

She'd wanted sex.

And then...

Life had happened.

Bringing her to this moment and the fact her car was on the way back with both of them in it.

Both of them.

She pushed her hand into her hair again. There were no more pins to dislodge, but there was quite a pile of them on the floor.

Micah heard a gravel crunch under car tyres.

The illusion of bravery that she'd been clinging to deserted her.

They were here.

Her heart jumped into her throat, and nerves made her spine tingle.

She smoothed imaginary wrinkles from her skirt, wondering if she had time to run upstairs to the bedroom and change clothes...for the fourth time today.

What did one wear to a planned seduction? Especially when the seduction was her own?

She walked through the house to greet them at the front door. She reached for the doorknob only to see it turn on its own.

She took a quick step back to avoid being flattened.

Captain Trent Williams filled the doorway.

Oh, Lord! He was taller, broader, more commanding than she ever remembered. His dark hair was cut military short, and, beneath his sage green T-shirt, she noticed his biceps rippled.

He was a hunk and a half in his military uniform and black boots. There was something about a man in uniform. She was all-but speechless already.

What on earth had she gotten herself into? And, criminy, don't let her out anytime soon.

He grabbed her by the shoulders and dragged her against his chest, crushing her. "Micah Collins, I presume."

She looked up. Her head spinning, unable to speak, unable to breathe, she had to settle to for nodding. His eyes, storm-tossed blue, commanded her attention.

He dug one hand into her hair, holding her steady. She didn't have time to blink before he kissed her.

Chapter Two

The kiss was hard and deep; and he didn't relent until she gave a little moan of surrender.

He tasted of power and determination, and he smelled of a rain-kissed night. His body was a solid mass of manhood, and she felt his cock against her. It was hard, too.

Her knees weakened. If his fingers weren't digging into her shoulders, she doubted she could have stood up.

"Well," Clayton said, closing the front door with a decisive thud and dumping two duffel bags on the hardwood foyer, "the messy awkwardness of the first kiss is out of the way."

Trent released her, slowly.

"I'm Clayton," the blond god said.

Micah shook her head, trying to focus on what the man had said. Her lips were swollen. She'd never been kissed like that before.

She realised Clayton had extended his hand. He stood just a few centimetres shorter than Trent, but Clayton was leaner. He resembled a long-distance runner, while Trent reminded her of a professional boxer.

She took Clayton's hand, and he clasped hers. His grip was comforting, as if he were a man who could be leaned on for support, either emotional or physical.

In a frightening situation, he'd be the one she wanted holding her. Trent, however, was the one she'd want brandishing a weapon to protect her.

"I'm the warm, tender one," Clayton said. He smiled, instead of glowering like his friend. "You've already met the insensitive half of this duo, Trent Williams."

Where Trent was intense, Clayton was more casual. His blond hair skirted regulation length, she was sure. But his eyes were his most engaging feature. They were the colour of bittersweet chocolate, and she could melt into their depths.

This could very well be the best ten thousand quid she'd ever spent. If she survived it. Well, she thought, her heart revving up with excitement, it might still be the best money she'd ever spent, even if she *didn't* survive it.

Her gravestone would read: She died happily in the service of her country.

"Share the joke?" Clayton asked.

"I was just wishing all my donations to military fundraisers had such rewards." Unconsciously, she touched her tender lips.

"And I was just wishing all of our assignments were this pleasant. Hey, Trent?"

Trent's answer was more of a grunt.

"A drink?" she asked.

"Irish whiskey," Trent said. "If you've got it."

"I do."

"Beer," Clayton said.

She headed for the kitchen, and Clayton followed. She pulled an already-opened bottle of Chablis from the wine cooler, and he took it from her.

"For you?"

"I'm a lightweight. One glass a night and no more."

"What happens if you have more?"

She closed the cooler with the toe of her shoe. "I get quite silly. Likely to do and say things I wish I hadn't."

"I'll keep that in mind. Where do you keep your wineglasses?" he asked.

"Getting me started early?"

"Absolutely."

She smiled. "Top shelf, in that cupboard to your right."

He kicked something as he moved towards the cupboard.

"Hairpin," she explained, feeling uncomfortable, exposed. "Might want to make sure you don't slip on any others."

He frowned in apparent confusion.

"Some people smoke or bite their nails."

"And you pull out hairpins."

"Right." Avoiding looking at him, she uncapped a beer and poured it into a mug.

"You yank them when you're nervous?"

"There's an even worse habit that you've already noticed." She'd dated before, and had managed to keep her little habit hidden from everyone. "I tend to leave them where they lay, as well."

"Micah?"

Topping off the beer, trying not to let it spill over the rim, she said, "Hmm?"

"Look at me."

She put down the bottle.

"We're both nervous, too."

Her mouth opened, and then she snapped it shut, afraid she'd look like an out-of-water fish otherwise.

After putting the wineglass on the granite countertop, he uncorked the bottle and splashed a small amount in it. He tasted the white wine before filling the glass. Was this a man after her own heart? Too bad she only had him for the weekend.

Earlier, forty-eight hours had seemed an absurdly long amount of time to have two men to ravish. Now it might just be a blink. In less than ten minutes, she'd been kissed nearly senseless and had a man look out for her drink. Lucky girl.

"You're the first one we've shared." Then he amended, "Well, at the same time, anyway." He touched her on the arm. "You're jumpy," he said.

Observant man.

"This might help take the edge off," he said, offering her the stem.

The glass was two-thirds full, a whole lot more than she drank on a usual basis.

"Wouldn't mind seeing you a bit silly, Micah."

She took a drink, but then he plucked the stemware from her hand and slid it back onto the countertop.

He advanced on her purposefully, but slowly, giving her time to move. But she was paralysed. She'd tasted Trent, now she wanted to taste Clayton.

With his lean, sexy body, he nudged her backward until she was against the cupboards.

"May I kiss you?"

So different from Trent. "Yes."

He laid one hand alongside her jawbone, capturing her. He feathered his other hand into her hair. "I'm glad you've already pulled out the pins," he said. "You saved me the effort."

She placed a hand on his chest. The top two buttons of his uniform shirt were open. He had a white T-shirt on beneath. With the way he was looking at her, she wanted to feel his bare skin. Would his chest be smooth or covered with downy-fine hair?

He brushed her lips with his own, in a light tease.

Oh. So delicious. Sensual.

He did it a second time, and then a third.

He teased until she demanded more.

She moved her hand behind his neck and drew him closer. Their tongues met and parried, and she leaned into him.

She'd had no idea what to expect when she'd made that huge donation in exchange for a weekend with the two soldiers. A little embarrassment, perhaps. Maybe even some hesitation or regret for being so impulsive. She'd even wondered if either of them would be unkind. After all, they were probably not happy to hear their services were needed in such an unusual way.

But each of them, each in their own unique way, chased away her inhibitions and made her respond so completely.

He tasted of mint and man, *and she wanted all of him.*

"What happened to the whiskey?"

Slowly, never taking his gaze from her, Clayton ended the kiss and responded, "Sorry, mate. We got distracted."

"You've never been distracted a day in your life," Trent said. "You're a captain in the Queens Royal Hussars. Nothing shakes you."

She felt a flush creep up her face. In less than five minutes, she'd been kissed by two men. Did life get any better? "I'll, uhm, just get that whiskey."

"She's a bit nervous," Clayton supplied.

"Do you swim, Micah?"

"Swim?"

He grinned, and it transformed his face, making him a whole lot less intense. "Swim. Like in the water," he said helpfully.

She nodded.

"Ever dipped in your toes and found the water too cold?"

"It's England," she said. "The water's always too bloody cold."

Clayton smiled.

"So what do you do about it?"

When she didn't answer right away, he crossed the room, almost silently. "Jump in," he supplied helpfully. "With both feet."

He unfastened her top button.

The calluses on his fingertips abraded her sensitive skin. "Well, that's certainly one way," she said.

"Ever done a ménage before?" Clayton asked, pouring Trent a whiskey, neat.

"Uh. No." Or a non-ménage, for that matter.

"Why us?" Trent asked, opening a second button.

"Trent—" Clayton warned.

Heat radiated from Trent's body, and there was a bite of spice to his aftershave. She scooted a little farther back, but the counter prevented her from moving more than a couple of milimetres. "Jaynie. You've probably met her."

"She's my sister's friend."

"She's a friend of mine, as well. And one night we were brainstorming ideas for the military fundraiser." She tipped her head back, determined to meet his gaze and not act like a simpering virgin. "She asked me what my wildest fantasy was. What I'd be willing to pay for."

"Over a glass of wine?" Clayton guessed.

"Well... Yes. And after a night with Brad Pitt, I said my second wildest fantasy was two sexy men. I actually never thought..." She smiled. "I never thought she'd put something together, then hit me up for the massive donation you two asked for."

"She…?" Trent asked.

"Jaynie said she'd found my two hunks, her words. And if I were willing to make a donation to the soldier's fundraiser, you two had wanted to spend a weekend with me. I could hardly refuse when all of you went to that effort. Queen and country, you know? All for a good cause."

"Methinks Jaynie has some explaining to do," Clayton said. He took a drink from his beer. "But I'm not complaining."

A third button surrendered beneath Trent's onslaught.

Her bra was visible, and her breathing changed, oxygen constricting deep in her chest.

He tugged the shirt's hem from her slim-fitting black skirt. Then, while his gaze continued to hold hers, he released the last two buttons.

"Uh…"

"You have to get wet when you go swimming," Trent told her. He grabbed her hand and put it on his cock.

Her eyes widened.

"Squeeze it," he said. "Harder."

She did.

"Now stroke."

Through his uniform pants, she did. She hoped he didn't realise how little experience she had pleasing a man.

"I want you naked," he said.

Here? In the kitchen?

He moved her hand away from his penis and then shucked the silky turquoise coloured blouse from her shoulders. The material swished to the tile, joining her hairpins.

"Turn around," he told her, backing off a couple of metres.

Feeling her own heartbeat in her throat, she did. Both men were watching her; she was hyper-aware of both of them. She suddenly wished she'd thought to turn on the radio or slide in a CD, any kind of music would be preferable to the sound of her ragged breathing.

Trent deftly released her bra, then lowered her skirt's zipper.

Trent worked the skirt past her hips and down her thighs. He knelt so she could step out of it. Surprising her, he folded the skirt then placed it on the countertop.

Micah had dressed for seduction, or for being seduced, as the case might be. She'd taken a trip to London for lingerie, and now she was terribly glad she had.

For the first time in her life, she was wearing a garter belt, stockings and a sexy thong. They were all black and lacy, and it was all a smart match with her bra.

She'd splurged on shoes, too. They were higher than she usually wore, and they had a spiky heel. The shoes made her calves actually look like they had a nice shape. No wonder so many women dropped a mint at the shops.

"Take off the bra," Clayton said.

Coming from him, the command was even more potent. She shrugged it off and let it pool to the floor.

Then she was mostly naked in front of two men, self-conscious and nervous.

"Beautiful," said Clayton. He moved in closer and cupped her breasts in his large palms, supporting their weight.

Capturing her gaze, he drew his thumbs across her nipples, teasing them until they became hardened, erect nubs. His touch was exquisitely wonderful, and her eyes shut, as if she could enjoy the sensations more that way.

She was aware on some level of Trent picking up his own whiskey glass and tossing back the amber liquid in a single swallow.

Her eyes opened again when Clayton brushed her lips with his.

"I'm afraid my mate will flatten me if I don't share."

It'd be more than fine with her if Clayton just swept her up the stairs and took her. For her first, she couldn't think of a more perfect man. But she had bought them both.

"Move behind her," Trent said.

Command dominated his tone. This was a man accustomed to being obeyed without hesitation. Nothing in his voice soothed; rather, it insisted.

"Take off your knickers," Trent told her.

He overwhelmed her senses.

Still, while Clayton moved away, she did. In for a penny...

Moments later, all she wore was a garter belt and stockings, along with her fabulous shoes. She resisted the impulse to strategically place her hands across her lower body.

Clayton got behind her. Reaching around, he cupped her breasts and started to play with her nipples again.

"Open your legs for me, Micah," Trent instructed. This time, he wasn't bossy. It sounded more like a request.

Again, she complied. Her throat was so dry, she could hardly swallow. *Wine.* A glass of wine would be great.

Clayton gently bit the tender flesh between her neck and shoulder while Trent got onto his knees.

She was captivated.

Trent licked a finger, then drew it across her clit.

Her knees threatened to buckle. Clayton, however, wasn't letting her go anywhere. He held her, supported her, kissing the side of her neck and keeping her overwhelmed.

Trent looked up at her and increased the pressure against her clit. He alternated pressure with long, sweeping strokes. She moistened. And as he dipped a finger into her vagina, she became totally wet.

He parted her labia and pressed on her clit.

"Ahhhh…" The man touched her exactly the way she liked, the same way she touched herself when she used her vibrator. "Just…" It would only take a few more minutes for her to come, especially with the way Clayton was tormenting her nipples.

This was all she had hoped for when she'd had a glass of wine and told Jaynie her wildest dreams. But never had she imagined it would be so exquisite. Two handsome, sexy men who were totally focused on her. Did life get any better?

Her hips jerked forward. "I'm—"

"Don't hold back," Clayton whispered in her ear. Then he nipped at her lobe.

His hands gripping her thighs, Trent moved in closer and licked her clit.

"Oh. Oh my… God!" This hot, hot man had his head between her legs!

"Come," Clayton told her.

Shaking convulsively, she did.

Trent didn't stop, even though she'd climaxed. He kept up the pressure, and then intensified it. It was a total assault. Her whole body felt as if it were on fire with desire. Nerve endings she didn't know she had were vibrating.

Deep inside, another orgasm built. She could hardly believe it was possible. She'd never come more than once. In fact, she generally just fell asleep after coming. But Trent was having none of that.

Clayton squeezed her breasts, moving them closer together.

Trent inserted one finger inside her before slipping in a second.

Her hands curled into his shoulders.

"You've got the hottest cunt," Trent said.

His words, raw and earthy, were enough.

She jerked convulsively, shamelessly. And then she screamed.

Clayton laughed, a seductive sound if ever there was one. His breath was warm on her skin. "It's my turn," he said. "I want to hear you scream for me."

Chapter Three

Clayton hadn't known what to expect when he'd agreed to Jaynie's suggestion. To tell the truth, he wasn't the type for one-night stands, and for the last couple of years, he'd focused on his career and being a good leader. He hadn't left any time for a relationship, and that was intentional. Too many military marriages failed. It took a special woman to marry a man and the Army.

Three years ago, he'd thought Sally might be that woman. They'd dated for almost a year, and he'd fallen in love with her sense of humour and insatiable sexual appetite. She was fiercely independent and dedicated to her job at an up-and-coming advertising agency. A match made in heaven, or so he'd thought.

When she'd asked when he was going to resign his commission, they'd had their first big row. She said she couldn't be involved with a man who would likely be sent overseas. She had cried. Tears he could deal with. The begging had been another thing entirely.

When none of that had moved him, Sally had thrown a piece of his grandmother's crockery against the wall. And he'd been finished with Sally. He'd put her in the car and driven her home. He hadn't answered a single telephone call or e-mail.

But now... Having a warm, willing woman in his arms... He suddenly realised what he'd been missing during his years of celibacy. Body armour and munitions only went so far. There really was no substitute for a woman's companionship, and for exploring the softness and suppleness of her body.

Sharing with Trent. Who knew? They'd done everything together since boyhood. Well, everything except sharing the same woman at the same time. And why not? They'd talked about it often enough. And to find a woman that wanted exactly that. What could be better?

He held her, supported her while Trent cajoled a third orgasm from her.

"I can't!" she said.

"Oh," Clayton whispered, "you can."

She arched and moaned. His cock throbbed in demand. No way masturbating would take this edge off. He needed to be deep inside her pussy. Or her mouth. He'd settle for being in her mouth.

Her body was becoming more compliant, and she was leaning on him more and more.

No worries from him, though.

He liked supporting her, holding her, kissing her, oh, right, and playing with her full, sensuous breasts. Her nipples were so responsive. The nibs were hard, and he was ready to have them in his mouth.

She groaned.

He squeezed her nipples hard at the same time Trent pulled her pelvis a bit more towards him.

"Trent! Clayton!"

She shuddered and shook. He grinned. This woman was going to be well satisfied before they even got her to bed. By the morning, she wouldn't be able to stand up.

He couldn't resist a pleased grin.

"I think our girl may need a bit of a rest, hey, Trent?"

From his place on his knees, he looked up at Micah.

"Yes," she whispered. "Mercy. Please."

Trent chuckled. The man was intense, that was for sure.

Slowly, Clayton released her. "Do you have a robe?"

"On my bed. Upstairs."

He went up the stairs and headed for the first open door. Nice house. Naturally, it would be. He couldn't forget she'd paid ten thousand quid for the weekend. Which made him wonder. She was attractive and charming. She could have a ménage with any men she wanted. She sure as hell didn't need to write a cheque for it.

He found a white, silky, frothy, see-through confection on her bed. This was a robe? It'd do little to keep her warm, and it would do even less to hide her charms. As if he needed his appetite whetted even further.

He returned to the kitchen to find her leaning against the counter, a glass of wine in hand. Trent was pouring his second whiskey.

But Clayton only had eyes for Micah.

Jesus, she was desirable.

Her big breasts were bare, her nipples still hard, the aureoles still red from where he'd squeezed her. Her breasts all but begged to be touched, held, cradled, fondled.

Trent had his head buried in her crotch earlier, and now Clayton was finally getting a view of her entire body.

Her hips were shapely, and the starkness of the black lingerie against the creamy softness of her thighs was startling. He'd never been a huge fan of frilly or fancy. He preferred naked women. But the sight of her could convince him to spend a month's pay on all things lacy and feminine.

The patch of dark hair between her legs hid the secrets he wanted exposed. Better get her covered up, now. "Here you are, love." He offered her the robe.

With a grateful smile, she put down her wine and accepted the robe. "Your beer must be warm by now."

"Small price to pay to hold you while you come. Again and again."

She slipped into the floor-length robe and tied a knot at the waist. He'd been right, it was transparent. But the best thing? With the way it fell and the folds of the fabric, it made her look even sexier.

It took all his self-control not to lift her up, sit her on the granite counter top and slam his cock into her.

Instead, he picked up the glass he'd all-but forgotten about, and then he said, "A toast."

"To?" Micah asked.

"New experiences?" Clayton suggested.

"Multiple orgasms," Trent said.

"Ugh. I'm not sure I can survive it!"

They clinked glasses, and Micah laughed.

"Hope we're worth your money," Trent said.

"Well... So far."

She looked down into her glass, as if to hide the furious blush that bloomed on her cheeks. Clayton wasn't sure he knew women who actually still blushed. He was captivated. "I'm going to kiss you again."

"Do you know how bad I want to fuck her?" Trent asked.

He could imagine coming home to her from a long deployment or even a long day. His groin tightened at the very idea. "You're going to wait," Clayton said, "until I kiss her." He plucked her stem from her fingers and put it on the counter beside his beer mug.

And he did. Kiss her.

She tasted of innocence and heat in one contradictory package. The wine was sweet on her tongue. Ending the kiss, he nipped at her lower lip. Maybe Trent was right. They could kiss later. Right now, his cock throbbed painfully, and he wasn't sure how much longer he could wait. "Upstairs," he told her.

"About damn time," Trent grumbled.

Clayton smacked her on the bum as she started up the stairs. She wasn't walking very fast as she took each step. One hand was curled on the railing. With the other, she held her wine as if for dear life.

"You've given this some thought," Clayton said, his hand resting proprietarily against the small of her back. He considered hanging back a bit so he could watch her arse as she climbed up. "How do you want to do this?"

She almost tripped up the stairs. "Uh. I was hoping you gentlemen would lead the way."

"I have an idea or two," Trent said. "And one of them includes your mouth and my cock."

When they arrived in the bedroom, she faced them both. "I have a confession to make before we go too much farther."

Oh, oh. Like why she was paying for sex?

She took a long drink from her wine. "There's another reason I agreed to Jaynie's suggestion. Why I wrote a cheque for ten thousand pounds." After another fortifying sip, she then drained her glass.

How bad was this confession going to be?

She put down the glass, then combed her fingers through her shoulder-length dark hair. If there'd been any pins there, she'd have sent them plummeting to the floor.

"I have a small problem."

Warning alarms sounded in Clayton's head. "Go on," he said.

"We have condoms," Trent said. "If it's an STD. We'll keep your secret."

Her eyes widened and she blinked. "No. It's not like that. Well, you see…" She took a breath and in a single exhalation said, "I'm a virgin."

"A virgin?" A twenty-something year old virgin? How the hell did that happen?

"I just didn't want to surprise whichever of you was the first to figure it out."

She was a virgin and one of them was going to relieve her of that burden. Christ. He'd been in combat, and he doubted he'd ever walked ground that was more laden with landmines.

"I hope you don't mind."

"Fuck." Trent said what Clayton was thinking.

"C'mon," Trent said. "We thought we were playing with someone who knew the score."

"My mother was ill for a lot of years," she said. "That didn't give me a lot of time for a social life." She curled her hand around Clayton's wrist. "I'm not a freak."

"No one said you were. Just…" This time, he was the one who ploughed his hand into his hair.

"I took care of my mother for years. I want to live. I want to make up for lost time."

"For God's sake, Micah. I don't go around deflowering virgins. *We* don't," he corrected at Trent's scowl.

"I paid you to do exactly that."

"Sorry."

"You're reneging?" she asked, licking her bottom lip.

"Oh, no you don't. I don't take guilt trips, Micah. Don't even try selling me one."

"Find yourself a nice boy who'll marry you and settle down."

"I would if that's what I wanted." She shook her head and dark strands of hair fell alluringly across her cheeks. "That's not what I want." Then she boldly grabbed Clayton's penis. "That's not what you want, either."

She was right on that score.

"Or you," she said, reaching for Trent.

"Micah," Trent warned.

She let go of Trent and said, "Take off your clothes."

Trent's mouth fell open. Two soldiers, both of them combat veterans, didn't have a clue what to do with one slight woman. Clayton would have laughed if the situation weren't so serious.

"I mean it. I made a huge donation to fuck you." She poked Trent in the chest and squeezed Clayton's cock extraordinarily hard.

He winced. The woman knew what she wanted and knew how to make a point.

"No STD's," she said, "no hang ups. Now take off your damn shirt."

Trent shot him a glance. "This was your idea, as I recall."

"Good of you to mention it." What a good mate, had his back, did he?

Her eyes narrowed. "I could ask for my money back."

"Lady, I'd give you every pence, happily," Trent said.

"I'd rather you kept your word, like a man."

She couldn't have landed a more direct hit if she'd been armed with a map. Questioning a soldier's integrity?

"You want to be fucked?" Trent demanded. The words were a growled warning. "It'll be my pleasure." He yanked his shirt from his waistband. "What're you waiting for? Take off that piece of fluff, get on your back and spread your legs."

"Bring it on, soldier." She let go of Clayton's cock and moved towards the bed.

"Unless you want to be fucked from behind. In that case, get on your hands and knees."

"Hang about," Clayton said.

Fury flashed in Trent's eyes.

And Clayton noticed that her eyes, which had been light blue, like a cloudless summer day, were now dark and stormy.

"Never mind trying to defuse the situation, even if you are a munitions expert," she said to Clayton. "I want you naked, too. I paid for the goods. Deliver them."

The woman might not be military, but she knew how to take precise aim when she fired a volley.

Despite her bravado, he noticed her fingers shaking as she undid the knot in her belt.

Trent unbuckled his belt and let it fall to the floor. It clanked on the hardwood plank.

Then he untied his boots and toed them off. He threw them; his socks followed.

How the hell had a fun evening gotten so far out of hand?

Oh yeah, Micah had questioned their integrity.

She proudly, bravely, stupidly dropped her robe. It fluttered to the floor. Trent's trousers landed on top. He was in boxers and a T-shirt. Micah wore only her shoes, the garter belt, and stockings with a seam up the back. Did she have any idea what she did to him, how much it took not to ravish her?

"Take off your clothes, Clayton," she said. "It's no different than it was downstairs."

"The hell it's not." His own anger began to simmer.

"The woman wants to be relieved of her virginity," Trent said. He tugged off his shirt. "Should take about five seconds."

Fuck.

She knew what she was doing, though, knew how to goad both of them. Damn her.

Her eyes were wide, but it wasn't with fear.

She evidently fed off the intensity.

In that regard, she wasn't all that different than him and Trent. Adrenaline was a powerful driving force. He understood why she was handling the situation this way. It beat fear and uncertainty. She'd get what she wanted on her terms, whether he liked it or not.

"Clayton?" she said.

What the hell was he supposed to do? Tell her to suck him off while his mate took her? Tension crawled up his back.

Chapter Four

She wasn't scared, even though she probably should be. She'd pulled the tiger's tail, and instead of running, she was standing there, facing him down.

Instead, she felt more alive than she ever had. Her mother hadn't wanted Micah being a caregiver. Mum had wanted Micah to hire a nurse, go out and enjoy life while she was still young. But Micah's sense of loyalty and her pure love for her mother made that impossible.

But now, she wanted every experience. Which was why she'd sky-dived last year and travelled to the Gobi Desert six months ago. Life was for living. And didn't she know it. Her mother had been robbed of too many years. That wouldn't happen to Micah.

These two men, warriors, heroes, had morals higher than she'd expected. She'd believed men were interested in a quick lay, no matter the circumstances. That they so vehemently objected had shocked her. When it didn't appear guilt would work, she'd gone for the jugular, attacking their honour.

To be honest, she admired their restraint.

Had she been a man, she'd be sporting a broken nose by now.

Trent removed his boxers. His cock was swollen, sticking straight out. It was bigger than she expected, much longer and thicker around. His balls were huge.

"I said spread your legs," Trent told her.

She feasted on adrenaline and nerves.

He was sexier without his clothes than he had been fully dressed. His chest was broad, his biceps cut with definition. He had a tattoo. Was it a dragon? Or something else?

She opened her legs wider, leaving her more exposed, more vulnerable. And she wouldn't trade it for anything.

He sheathed his cock with a condom, then stroked himself to full arousal.

A low fire ignited in her belly. She was going to take all of that? Was it even possible?

He climbed onto the bed and poised there.

He began to ease his cock inside her. She was so dry, she winced.

Trent froze, then he backed up. "You're not wet enough."

"Let me," Clayton said.

Trent got out of the way. Still fully dressed, Clayton moved between her legs and began to lick her cunt.

She writhed, responding to his touch. He was gentler than Trent had been, but just as sexy. She dug the heels of her shoes into the mattress and arched, seeking more.

He gave it.

She hadn't known either of them long, but she was relieved Clayton wasn't being standoffish.

Her pussy was moist. Unbelievably, even after all the orgasms Trent had given her downstairs, she was close to coming again.

Apparently realising how wet she was, Clayton climbed off the bed. Probably wouldn't be for long, though, as he was untying his shoes.

Yes! So close to getting what she wanted.

Trent got back into position. His eyes were intense, dark. His jaw was clenched, and a vein throbbed in his temple.

He stroked his cockhead across her clit. She arched, seeking more. Slowly, he gave it to her.

"Tell me what you want."

"You."

"Tell me what you want," he repeated, the words tight, as if forced through gritted teeth.

"I want your cock."

"Where?"

"In my pussy."

"Ask for it," he said.

"Please," she said, gasping as he went deeper. "I want your cock in my pussy."

Clayton, his lithe body naked, climbed on the bed. He captured her head and closed his fist in her hair, holding her fast. He claimed her mouth.

She was overwhelmed.

Sensation after sensation rocked her world.

Trent thrust deep, tearing her hymen. Clayton swallowed her cry. Then he intensified his kiss. Slowly, as she adjusted to him, Trent began to move back and forth, pumping into her, then pulling back out.

Clayton ended their kiss, then bent to suckle on one of her breasts. She couldn't take it. Couldn't think. Couldn't— She needed...

Clayton sucked one nipple into his mouth and bit it while brutally pinching the other.

Arching her back, she screamed.

Trent stopped, letting her ride out her orgasm, grinding against his pelvis.

"You like it a little rough," Clayton said.

"Yes." She tried to turn her head away, but he wouldn't let her. He kept her gaze captive.

"Tell me about when you masturbate."

"I…"

"We just took your virginity. No shyness."

"I use clamps on my nipples."

"Where are they?"

"I—" She gave up. These two were as relentless as she was. "Top drawer of my dresser. Beneath the knickers."

"Ever been spanked?" Trent asked her.

Her eyes widened.

"You use clamps," he observed.

"I've never been spanked," she said, barely able to breathe as he began to move inside her again.

This time, he felt good. She liked the way he stretched her and filled her, rode her.

"You've wondered, though. About being spanked."

"What is this, true confession time?"

"You've got forty-eight hours. How you want to spend them is your choice. What will you wonder about next week, next year? Your choice if you want regrets."

"Anything I want?"

"Ask," he told her. "We can say no."

"Fuck me harder."

He grinned. He no longer looked so ferocious. "That," he said, "I can do."

"I want you on your side," she said

He pulled out and repositioned her on her left side. "Put your right leg over my hip."

She blinked. "Uh…I'm not a contortionist."

172

"Trust me."

The position left her a bit uncomfortable, but she did as he asked.

"Do you need lube?"

"I'm good. Well, for being in this position."

"Good, now see if you can get one of your hands behind my neck to hold on."

"Didn't we have the gymnastics discussion?" Despite her complaints, she did as he told her. Each shift opened her up a little, gave him a different angle. She felt so full, so penetrated.

"And from that position, you can open your mouth and suck on my cock."

Clayton's words gave her an instant thrill. She expected Trent to be a little crude, but when Clayton did it, it had a way of twisting her insides into a knot of wanton desire.

"Open your mouth," he said again.

She did.

And since they already knew she was a virgin, she didn't need to tell him she'd never sucked cock before.

He filled her mouth while Trent thrust deep in her vagina.

She moaned at his depth, and her moan opened her mouth wider for Clayton's penetration.

This...

This was beyond anything she'd imagined.

Clayton tasted of soap with a slight hint of salt. He held her head steady as Trent moved his hips. "Be careful with your teeth," he warned. "The most sensitive spot is at the top of my cock, just beneath the head. If you can put some pressure there with your tongue, you'll be doing everything right."

She nodded.

"You said you wanted to be fucked harder," Trent said. Then he did.

Oh. Oh.

He drove into her, impaling her.

He was impossibly deep. It felt so powerful. It hurt. It was dizzying.

He pushed against her womb, and her moans were muffled by Clayton's cock stuffed in her mouth.

Trent never went for a rhythm she could figure out and accommodate.

He stroked hard and deep, then more shallow. She arched and bent, asking for more, seeking more, and he gave it with a powerful slam.

She was going to come undone. Her body convulsed; Clayton took full advantage of it, getting more and more of his cock in her mouth. Unbelievably, his cock got harder.

"I'm going... Going... To come," he warned her. His words were incoherent and broken. His breathing was ragged. "Micah!" He pulled out of her mouth. He groaned. Moaned. Called out her name.

He jacked himself off, his semen landing on her face in warm spurts that made her feel naughty.

Trent continued to fuck her. His motions were jerky and uneven. Rational thought fled. When Clayton swiped some of his cum from her cheek and fed it to her, she sucked on his fingers, licking them clean.

The sensations were too overwhelming for her to climax.

But Trent dragged her backward, holding her hips prisoner as he drove in deeper.

He came with a quiet, "Fuck *me*."

The two men were so completely different, even in the way they came. One loud, one restrained.

"How are you feeling?" Clayton asked.

"My pussy is tender."

"Fucked you hard enough?"

She wiggled, wishing she could see him. Cheekily, she said. "Yes. That'll do for now."

Trent slapped her exposed right buttock hard.

"Ouch!"

"That's just the beginning."

"What?"

"If you think you're getting away with questioning our integrity, Micah Collins —"

"You're not serious!" She tried to face him, but he kept her prisoner. He wouldn't. Not really. Even though he'd just asked her about spanking, he wouldn't paddle her as punishment. He'd simply use it as a way to tease her into greater arousal, wouldn't he?

"Completely serious," he affirmed.

His left hand was on the back of her neck. His right hand was on her buttocks. He held her firmly. "You'd spank me now after you just... *After we had sex?*"

"After you manipulated us?" he corrected. "In short, yes."

"Clayton?" Desperately, she looked around for him. But the more tender of the two shook his head. Damn him. He wasn't going to come to her rescue.

"You crossed a line, Micah."

A slow tendril of fear uncoiled in her gut.

They were both honourable, she knew that. But they were still men. Men who wouldn't tolerate her shenanigans. While she might protest, she couldn't be happier. She hadn't dated much, and the men she had dated had been really easy to railroad. She'd hated that. Even Clayton, the kinder one, had his limits.

Before she knew what was coming, Trent had moved them both. From the moment he arrived, she'd recognised him as a powerful man, a warrior deserving of respect. Now she was seeing him as a righteously angry man. And she was deserving of his punishment.

And now he was sitting up in her bed, and she'd gone arse end over teakettle. She was across his lap, her bottom upturned, and she was dragging her legs together, trying to close her thighs to maintain some sort of dignity.

Dignity, she knew, was the first thing he'd have off her.

Chapter Five

"How many do you deserve?"

Trent waited patiently for her answer. When the situation called for it, he could wait quietly for hours. And looking at the swell of her arse, the curve of her hips and hearing her ragged breaths could amuse him endlessly. She wouldn't have the tolerance for that, though, he already knew that about her.

In fact, the more he knew about her, the more he appreciated her.

He liked a cheeky woman who would keep him on his toes. He liked a woman who knew what she wanted and would do anything to get it.

He and Clayton had spent a long time together over the past dozen or so years that they'd been friends. They'd each had girlfriends. Clayton had come close to being serious with Sally. Trent wasn't as smart as his comrade. He'd actually proposed to Deena. Good thing he got out before she got a ring, the equivalent of a noose, around his neck.

Only, luckily, he'd come to his senses. She wouldn't stand up to him. Her manipulations weren't transparent like Micah's. Deena was subtle, and she was a liar. About anything, anytime. How to tell if Deena was lying, his sister had teased. Her lips were moving.

He sure as sunshine didn't need a woman back at home he couldn't trust.

This one, though, with her arse begging for his punishment, wouldn't lie about anything, not even a tiny lie, he was sure. "I'm waiting for your answer," he told her.

"What's the regular sort of number for something like this? Three?"

He laughed. "Clayton?"

"Twenty."

"Twenty?" She strained against the hand Trent had on her neck, trying to raise her face a little. He pushed her back down. "Are you mad?" she demanded. Her face might be buried in the bedspread and her voice muffled by the mattress, but Miss Rich Girl who could buy two soldiers for the weekend was still being the county princess and letting her outrage be known.

Little did she know her outrage had barely started. "You don't think twenty is a bit harsh?"

"Thirty," Clayton said.

"Twenty it is," Trent said. "Ten from each of us?"

"Clayton wouldn't!"

"Ten from each of us," Trent affirmed. "Just a suggestion, vixen. Dig in your knees a bit and lift your bum a bit more."

"So you can hit it harder? Mad. You're mad."

Maybe. But he could smell the scent of her arousal. And the way she was wiggling, she was trying to grind her pussy against his thigh. *The lady doth protest too much.* "It will hurt less," he told her, "if you take the blows across your buttocks rather than your thighs, but if that's your wish…"

"No!" She did as he told her, getting into position.

He landed the first smack across her arse cheeks. She wiggled, but said nothing. He gave her three more in quick succession, and that elicited small moans. "How many is this?"

"At least a dozen!"

He met Clayton's gaze. They both grinned at her expense. "This is number five." He delivered it smartly and she moaned. "Why are you getting spanked, Micah?"

"For manipulating you."

"For trying to manipulate us," he corrected. "To make sure it doesn't happen again."

"Yes, sir."

"Ought to add extra for impertinence."

"Sorry! Honestly!"

He enjoyed the feel of his hand on her bare flesh. "You arse is getting red," he said.

"That's because you're beating me."

He laughed, then his hand connected with her flesh two more times. She was getting hot, and bothered, if her moans were anything to go by. It hurt, he knew that, but he guessed that the sensations in her body and the neurons firing in her brain only made her more aroused.

She'd be very much aware of her naked body exposed to their gaze, and she'd be feeling the dampness between her legs. She'd probably be fervently praying that neither of them would notice how wet she was.

"Spread your legs a bit," Clayton told her.

She hesitated for a couple of seconds before complying.

"Better view of her cunt?" Trent asked.

"And how slick she is. One would think she might be enjoying it."

This time, her moan did sound miserable. He could almost feel sorry for her. Almost.

"Continue on," Clayton told Trent.

He finished her off with the three remaining slaps and then said, "Your turn, I believe."

"Get on your hands and knees," Clayton told her. "And don't move."

She did as she was told, and the sight of her, the scent of her made Trent's cock stir again. That shouldn't be possible, but there it was.

He moved out from beneath her, then went to her bathroom to get rid of the used condom and to get her a warm flannel.

When he returned, he gently washed her, and it was only a moment or two before Clayton delivered another command. "Put your forehead on the mattress."

She did.

So, Clayton wasn't going for an across-the-lap spanking, then. This might be really interesting

"Arch your back." He spoke quietly, but there was no misunderstanding his focus and intent.

Trent grabbed his cock and began working it. He'd figured it would be interesting, this ménage. But he'd had no idea how turned on he'd be watching another man pleasure the woman who'd already crawled under his skin.

"Get your arse a little higher in the air."

"Clayton," she said softly, "I thought…"

"You thought wrong, love. I didn't want Trent to fuck you like that. You're going to be spanked for torturing me."

"But that's what I wanted," she protested.

"And you got what you wanted. And now I will, too."

Clayton's voice was ragged and raw with emotion. Seems neither of them had gotten what they bargained for when Jaynie cornered them at the pub.

"Open your legs a bit more. " He slapped her on that tender flesh on the underneath of her arse cheek. She wiggled around.

He caught her on the other leg.

Then he grabbed her hip bones and dragged her back, burying his face in her cunt.

Blood rushed to Trent's cock. She liked getting spanked. He liked spanking her. And, equally as well, he liked watching her be spanked.

She shamelessly pushed back, seeking more from Clayton.

Instead of giving her what she wanted, Clayton moved away and gave her a few more spanks, falling randomly on her buttocks, not where she was expecting them.

While Trent watched, Clayton dipped two fingers in her vagina and finger fucked her.

"I want..."

"You may not come," Clayton said.

And somewhere along the line, Trent had gotten the reputation of being the hard ass of the duo?

Clayton licked her, pressed on her clit, made her moan.

The sixth and seventh spanks were more intense. "You understand what this is about, correct?"

"Yes! You're torturing me."

Trent cupped his balls with his hand. They were full and swollen again. The idea of being in one of her holes was becoming an insistent demand.

The eighth made her yelp.

He went back to finger fucking her. Even from the distance, Trent could see the slick dampness of her pussy juices.

Using her own moisture as lubricant, Clayton began to work a finger into her anus.

"I—"

"You can take it," Clayton told her.

"And you want to," Trent said. "You want it all, you said. All the experiences."

"Yes! But—"

"Bear down."

"Clayton!"

"You're not getting out of this, love." He pulled out his finger and eased it in again. "Bear down."

She was fussing and struggling, and Trent caught the unspoken command in his mate's nod. Coming closer, he slapped her right arse cheek, hard.

"Argh!"

But the distraction was enough. She moved to escape, and in the process, her arse opened up. Clayton slid his finger in, to the hilt.

He grabbed a tube of lube from the nightstand with his free hand. Trent, always ready to help a fellow soldier, took the tube and flipped up the cap. He squirted a huge dollop that Clayton used to prime her with a second finger.

"You've still a good slap to go," he told her.

"I think I'm coming apart from the inside."

She wasn't the only one.

Now that Trent had met her, now that he'd tasted her, experienced her, he wanted more. Tonight, even forty-eight hours, wouldn't be enough. He doubted it would be for her, either.

At Clayton's nod, Trent gave her a stinging, painful tenth spank.

"Do not come," Clayton told her.

"Mean!"

"Love, hang about. If you think me denying you this orgasm is mean, just wait."

Trent climbed on to the bed. He couldn't wait for the next few minutes.

Chapter Six

Clayton gently withdrew his finger from her arse. He didn't need to tell her to put Trent's cock in her mouth; she naturally did it. Things were easy between them, as if they'd been doing it for years. One thing was certain, he didn't want this to end.

While her body was in a different position, he took the opportunity to open the vicious little jaws of her nipple clamps. Her breasts hung down naturally, and her nipples were still peaked. This would be easy and would catch her completely off guard. The pain, the fact she was sucking off Trent, the stinging sensation on her arse, it would all work together to distract her brain when he took her anally.

Trent, seeing what Clayton was about, pushed his hands into her hair.

Clayton reached beneath her and fondled her breasts.

"You drive me wild," she told him, coming off Trent's cock for just a moment.

Clayton tweaked her nipples a little. She wiggled and all but purred contentedly. Then, surprising her, he clamped one nipple with the metal jaws.

She raised her head.

"Breathe into it," he told her.

"But..."

While she was busy protesting, he fastened the other nipple clamp in place.

She hissed a breath in through her clenched teeth.

"Suck me," Trent told her.

"It hurts."

"Give it twenty seconds," Trent said. "And in the meantime, woman, *suck my dick.*"

Clayton sucked on her clit while she followed Trent's order.

Her clit was swollen. Another time, maybe he'd clamp it, too. Her reaction would be worth every moment. He doubted he'd ever known a more sensual, responsive woman.

When her breathing was a little more normal, when she'd adjusted to the lack of blood flow to her nipples, he finger fucked her pussy and her arse.

Minutes later, her breaths became little ragged bursts, and her climax was close. Clayton took that opportunity to press his cock against her tightest hole.

He eased in a bit, stroking her back, telling her, "Bear down. Relax."

With her mouth full of Trent, all she could do was moan.

"Bear down. Almost there." He clenched his back teeth together. He couldn't believe he was ready for her again. He was almost ready to explode.

Trent pulled on her nipple clamps, and Clayton shoved the rest of the way in.

Micah let out a muffled scream.

"You're there," he told her.

She remained frozen.

"There," he repeated. "You're doing great." Heaven help him. It wasn't possible to feel this way about a woman he'd just met. He'd had a taste, and he wanted more. Her arse was so tight, and after the years of celibacy...

Trent suddenly pulled back and spurted on her breasts. When Clayton watched Trent come all over her, he almost went over the edge.

"So full," she said. Her words sounded almost dreamy, far away.

Clayton went back to what worked though, and tried to detach the way he'd learned if he were to ever be taken prisoner and interrogated. Detach. Detach.

"Come in me," she said.

Training? What training?

Micah's demand shoved him over the edge. She could wrap him around her little finger. And had.

He came, pumping her full.

Shocking him, she climaxed, too.

Was there another woman for him? For them?

* * * *

"One of you has to carry me to the shower."

"You're assuming one of us has enough energy to carry you," Clayton said.

"You're soldiers. You've got inner resources. One of you has to carry me." After Clayton had climaxed and she'd ridden out the waves of her own orgasm, she'd rolled to her side. Somehow, she'd ended up between the two men. They were both facing her, and they were all three tangled together.

She'd never known it was possible to be this content. Maybe that's why she hadn't dated much. Maybe she was waiting.

Or maybe she was being ridiculous.

This could be just a forty-eight hour interlude for them. She shouldn't make it into anything more. No matter how tempting. They were military men, under the best of circumstances, a relationship with a soldier wasn't an easy thing.

"Right then," Trent said, always the one to take charge, "into the shower with us all." He climbed from bed, then swept her into his arms. To Clayton, he said, "You can bloody well walk yourself."

She giggled as she snuggled against his chest.

Since his arms were full, Clayton had to turn on the shower water. "I'll wash your front," she told Clayton, "if you'll wash my back," she said to Trent.

"Might be hard to resist taking you," he said. "After watching Clayton have a go at you..."

"I don't think I could stand up."

"Maybe we should find out."

Trent nuzzled her neck while she rose on tiptoes to kiss Clayton in a nothing-held-back open-mouth kiss.

One of them must have reached for the soap, because her entire body was suddenly slick. "Where do you get your energy?"

Trent said, "You're addictive."

He slid soapy hands across her body then knelt to kiss the small of her back.

"Tomorrow may not be enough," Clayton said.

"Thank God!"

Trent answered more earthily, by guiding his penis between her legs.

She couldn't... But the soap, the water, the heat, the soldiers...

"It's not easy," Clayton said, "being military."

"It isn't easy," she said, "losing your family."

"Touché," Trent added, with a gentle forward motion of his hips.

"It isn't easy," she continued, "wondering *what if*, instead of going for it."

"You know," Trent said. "I would have done this for nine thousand quid."

She would have turned, but with their positions, it was impossible. Instead, she bumped her hips back a bit, hinting at what he might get, if he behaved, and when her bum stopped hurting.

She'd never felt more gloriously alive. And she was looking forward to the rest of the weekend and possibly her life with her two brave soldiers.

"Maybe even eight," he amended.

"Yes, well, I believe I'll be writing Jaynie a cheque of my own," said Clayton.

After all, it was for a good cause.

FROM THE RUINS

Bronwyn Green

Dedication

In loving memory of my Grandparents, Ruby Green and Harold Bartz. Your love was the epitome of Happily Ever After. Thank you for showing our family what's important in life. I miss you both so much.

Thanks to the Torrid Tartlets – Brynn, Carol and Lacey – you guys rock. I'd also like to thank the FNMS – Chel, Jen, Cheryl, Marti and Mary. Thank you also to my amazing editor Claire, and to Matt, Mom, Cait, Manda, Margaret and Julie. I couldn't ask for better friends or family.

Chapter One

"Where are you going? I just got here."

Moira Boulton and her friend, Bethan, stopped on the stairs of the USO dance hall and stared at the handsome stranger with the American accent and the glacier-blue eyes. Her breath stalled in her chest as she met his gaze. She would have thought that eyes the colour of a winter sky would be cold and remote, but not his. Fiery and intense, his gaze raked over her body, sending tingles coiling through her middle.

Despite his overly forward behaviour, her lips twitched in amusement. "I'm sorry, sir, but do we know each other?"

Flashing her a devastating smile, he bowed slightly, his burnished brown hair drooping over his forehead. "I'm Private David Webber of the United States Army, and if I'm not mistaken, you're the mother of my future children."

His companions whom she'd barely noticed chuckled good naturedly as a startled laugh escaped her. "The mother of your children, you say?"

"Well, future children," he said with a wink.

"How often does that line actually work?"

"I don't know. You're the only one I'm ever going to say it to."

He obviously wasn't serious, but he was charming. Shaking her head in bemusement, she offered him her hand. "I'm Moira Boulton and this is my friend, Bethan Jones."

He nodded politely to her friend as his large, warm hand closed around Moira's. "Will you give me the honour of the next dance?" he asked. "After all, we have a wedding to plan."

For a moment, she imagined the sensation of laying her head against his broad chest and feeling his strong arms around her. It was tempting to return to the loud, crowded hall, but she needed to get home. "The last bus is leaving shortly, and we need to be on it."

His disappointment appeared genuine, but how could it be? After all, they'd just met. "I'm sure there are plenty of other girls inside who would love to dance with you," she said as she pulled her hand free, ignoring the sour feeling in her stomach as she imagined Mary Katherine Landis in his arms.

He frowned waving away the suggestion and cocked his head towards the open door of the dance hall. "Give me your hand."

There was something about this man that encouraged her trust. Even if Bethan hadn't been there, she'd still feel safe with him, but somehow that same sense of trust left her feeling somewhat unnerved. They were in the middle of a war, for God's sake, not to mention the fact they didn't know one another. But as she studied his open expression, she realised she wanted to know him. Taking a leap of faith, she placed her hand in his again and allowed him to lead her to the walk-way at the bottom of the stairs.

A lively tune drifted from the building along with the scent of cigarette smoke, and David gently pulled her into his arms. "At least give me the pleasure of a dance until your bus arrives."

She glanced around the street. "Here?"

He gestured to the darkening sky. "The moon is almost full, and the stars seem nearly close enough to touch. But you're still the most beautiful sight here."

Following his lead, she swayed to the faint strains of music. "You're a right charmer, Mr. Webber."

"David," he corrected smoothly. "And I only speak the truth."

She had no doubt she was nothing more than a passing fancy for him. After all, he was stuck in a foreign country, and she was a diversion. As handsome and charming as he was, she was likely one of many such diversions. The question was, did she care? Despite Bethan's disapproving stare, Moira melted into David's warm embrace.

He tucked her hair behind her ear as he stared into her eyes. "You're a hard woman to catch, Moira."

She frowned. "Beg your pardon?"

"I've been trying to meet you for the last three weeks, but every time I make it to the hall, you're getting on that damnable bus."

Moira laughed, shaking her head.

"It's true. I snuck out early tonight in hopes of at least one dance with the most bewitching woman I've ever seen."

His compliments warmed her, false though they might be. "You do tell a lovely tale."

Shaking his head, he leaned towards her, his lips hovering above hers. "And you're stubborn," he muttered. "You ought to know, I'm about to kiss you."

"I should hope so," she breathed.

193

His lips brushed across hers, the barest of touches. With a soft caress, he cupped her cheek as he deepened the kiss. Opening against the gentle press of his mouth, her lips parted and welcomed the slight stroke of his tongue against hers. He tasted of coffee and rich, warm male.

For a moment, she forgot they were on a public street. She forgot that they'd only just met. She forgot everything but the pleasure of his kiss and the shelter of his embrace.

"Moira!" Bethan snapped, breaking the blissful spell David wove around her. "The bus is coming."

David raised his head, regret plain in his gaze. "When can I see you again?"

She glanced at the approaching vehicle, torn between the desire to stay and the relief that she couldn't. "I don't know."

"Be here tomorrow night."

She took a step back, sanity trickling back. "How do I know you'll be here?"

Releasing his hold on her, he unbuckled the brown leather band of his wristwatch and pressed the timepiece into her hand and held it there. "My sister gave this to me before I shipped out."

Moira tried to follow his logic, but shook her head in confusion.

A warm smile curved the lips that had so recently been on hers. "She told me she'd kill me if I came home without it. "I'll be back because I have to get my watch. And you'll be here so you can return it to me." Gently, he brushed her hair from her eyes. "I'll be here to see you, because I can't go home without it."

Clearly pleased with his logic, he dropped another kiss on her upturned mouth.

"How do you know I won't sell it in the meanwhile?"

"You won't," he said as he brushed his thumb over her cheekbone. He gave her another quick kiss and walked her to the open door of the bus.

David watched as Moira boarded the vehicle and held his gaze through the grimy window. He ignored the glare her friend aimed at him through the same dirty glass. He'd taken a big chance tonight, but he knew he could trust Moira, the same way he knew she was the woman he was going to marry.

He'd always laughed at his father and aunts when they'd insisted that they just 'knew' things. He could never imagine simply acting on a feeling instead of a carefully contemplated idea. It had always boggled his mind. Then he'd seen Moira, and he knew. He just *knew*. It had been far more than her beauty — though she was certainly lovely. He'd simply sensed that she was the one. So like a man possessed, he'd desperately tried to meet her. He'd taken nothing but razzing from the guys in the barracks ever since he'd seen her three weeks ago. He glanced at his friends where they still leaned against the railing watching the bus rumble away. They weren't laughing now.

Tonight he'd fall asleep with the taste of her on his mouth and the memory of her warm curves in his arms. The lilt of her low, sweet voice still wrapped around him, and he knew he'd hear her in his dreams. He finally had a voice to go with the deep brown eyes and full lips that had haunted every waking thought since he'd first seen her. He sighed, wishing they'd had more time tonight.

"C'mon, Davey," his friend Martin called nodding towards the open door of the Wood Street dance hall. "Let's get a beer for you and a woman for me."

Chapter Two

David hurried away from camp. His shoulders throbbed in pain but not as much as his thumb. So distracted by the idea of seeing Moira tonight, he'd missed nail heads more than once. But, his company had completed two more barracks to house the massing Allied Forces as they prepared their offensive against the Germans. Because of the hilly, rocky terrain, Wales had been deemed the perfect place to camouflage the growing number of troops. Soon, he'd join those soldiers, trading his hammer and saw for a gun and ammunition. Worry nagged at him. He was used to ploughing fields and mucking out stalls—not killing men. He was a long way from his family's farm in Michigan.

His gut tightened with anticipation as he crested the Wood Street hill and saw the shadowed figure of a woman pacing outside the dance hall. She was there. Even from this distance, he knew it was Moira. He could tell by the silky fall of her long sable hair and the enticing sway of her full hips.

"Moira," he called as he lengthened his stride.

She spun to face him, her skirt swirling around her, and his hands itched to stroke her silk clad legs. As he reached her, he pulled her into his arms, burying his face in her hair.

"I missed you," he said. Breathing deeply, his lips brushed across her cheek to her ear and the sharp tug of desire pulled at his middle. "You smell so good."

"I wasn't sure you'd come," she whispered as she pressed his watch into his hand.

He raised his head and stared into her beautiful, dark eyes. "Did you really think I'd miss the chance to see you again?" he asked as he buckled the strap around his wrist.

She shrugged and brushed her lips over the hollow at the base of his throat. When he caught his breath she giggled and did it again. He cupped her cheek and brushed his thumb over her cheekbone tilting her head back.

"You're playing a dangerous game, Miss Boulton."

She tried to squelch a smile. "And what game is that, Mr. Webber?"

Her smile faded as she looked into his heated gaze. God, he wanted her. It was crazy to think he could be so affected by someone he'd just met, but it was the truth. He'd wanted other women before, hell, he'd had other women before, but no one had tied him in knots like Moira did.

"What game is that?" she repeated in her lilting Welsh accent.

His thumb moved to trace the outline of her parted lips. His cock jerked at the catch of her breath as he slowly lowered his head.

"Teasing the hungry beast," he whispered against her mouth before he claimed it.

And he was hungry. For her. She tasted like honeyed tea with a sweetness that was all Moira. She drove her fingers through his hair and her lips parted beneath his. He swallowed her soft sigh as he pulled her closer. She shyly stroked his tongue as he delved into her mouth, sighing as he tasted her fully.

She pressed into him and her lush breasts flattened against his chest and cock hardened almost instantly. His arousal pressed against her and she stiffened in surprise. He pulled back, not wanting to frighten her. "I'm sorry, Moira. I—"

She bit her lower lip. "I'm not," she finally whispered.

His eyes widened and his mouth dropped open, but the ominous sound of propellers cut the quiet night. Pulling Moira into his arms, he scanned the sky as the scream of an air-raid siren drowned out all other sound. A bomb hit directly behind the dance hall and shook the cobblestone street where they stood. Flames lit the darkness and panicked screams filled the air.

He grabbed Moira's hand and dragged her across the street. They ran through abandoned yards, tearing through weathered gorse as he tried to get her as far as possible from the fires that were devouring the all wooden structures in its path.

"We need a place with a cellar," he panted as they ran.

"The church, but it's locked." She glanced over her shoulder, her eyes wide with fear. Another bomb exploded as it hit the ground near the street where he'd kissed her a few moments earlier.

That unnerving sense of knowing prickled across the back of his nape. Stopping their mad dash, he pointed at what used to be a fieldstone building, more precisely at the cellar doors that were only partially covered with rubble. "What was that?"

She squinted in the direction he pointed. "It used to be a pub."

Hopefully the basement would still be intact. Heart pounding in his chest, he switched directions and pulled Moira towards the ruins.

"David," she panted. "What are you—"

He pulled her to the ground and motioned for her to stay there. "Saving your life. Stay down."

He began to throw aside rocks and rubble, clearing the top of the doors. Disregarding his directive, she did the same as bombs continued to rain down on the city. Grunting, he shoved aside a charred wooden beam. "Found it." He yanked open the cellar door and pulled his flashlight from his belt, shining the thin shaft of light into the yawning darkness.

The steps looked solid. He tested them then turned back to Moira and tugged her in after him. Herding her into the dank, blackness, he pulled the door shut behind them. Another explosion rocked them, and they nearly fell down the remaining stairs. When they reached the hard-packed dirt floor, he shined the beam of light around the cramped space. A doorway framed with heavy wooden planks led into what looked like a wine cellar.

Taking her hand, David led her into the narrow room, still filled with bottles and barrels. At least they wouldn't die of thirst while they were down here. He ran the beam of light over shelves that had been dug into the earthen walls. Nothing but empty flour sacks. He shone the light over the walls again. Even before the above ground structure had been destroyed, the electricity had never been run into the cellar—which meant there might still be candles or an oil lamp down here. He felt around beneath the sack cloth until he found what he was looking for. A few candles and small box of matches as another bomb hit the ground above them, and the bottles rattled ominously.

"Are you sure it's safe here?" she asked.

He lit the partially burned candle and switched off his flashlight. Who knew how long they'd be down here. It was best to conserve the batteries.

He turned to face her. The candle's flame set their shadows to dancing on the walls and he saw the worry etched in her face. "It's better than staying above ground. I didn't want to risk your safety like that."

She pressed her lips together and nodded nervously as she pulled the flour sacks off the shelf and spread them on the floor. Sitting down she patted the ground next to her. "We may as well get comfortable," she said.

Their thoughts were obviously following the same path. Who knew when the shelling would stop? Sometimes it lasted minutes, other times, hours. Sitting at her side, he slipped his arm around her and gave her what he hoped was a reassuring squeeze. She startled as another barrage of shells hit the city above. He wrapped both arms around her and she buried her face in his chest.

"It'll be all right." He smoothed his hand down her back, in an attempt at comfort.

Raising her head, she looked into his eyes. "Kiss me," she said, her voice trembling. "Please."

David looked at the woman at his side. The flickering candlelight danced off her silky black hair and shimmered in her deep brown eyes. She didn't need to ask twice. He lifted her chin and covered her full lips with his own.

Wrapping her arms around his neck, she drew him down to the rough cotton covering the floor. He'd intended to leave some distance between their bodies, but now that her lush breasts were pressed against his chest, he couldn't bring himself to move. He'd never wanted a woman more. Her body fit him perfectly. He could only imagine how her soft curves would cradle him as he thrust into her.

As much as he wanted her, he forced what was left of the gentleman in him out of hiding. "Moira, I can't do this."

Hurt flashed through her wide, guileless eyes. "You don't want me?"

Shifting to his knees, he laughed — a half desperate sound and scrubbed his fingers through his hair. "Christ, yes, I want you. I want so badly I can't sleep at night. I imagine what it would be like to make love with you — to pleasure you until you cry out my name. But I can't."

She rose to her knees and faced him. Her arms crossed over her chest, drawing his attention to her full breasts — breasts that until recently had been pressed against him. "Are you married?" she demanded.

"What? No. Of course not." He sighed, not wanting to give words to his fear — to give it any kind of credence. "Soon, I don't know when, but I'll be joining the rest of the troops in France."

She moved her hands to her hips, tapping her fingers in annoyance. "Were you planning to leave tonight?"

He was slow to answer, not sure what she was driving at. His brow furrowed. "No."

"If you want me, and you're neither married nor leaving tonight, why won't you touch me?" She pursed her lips in frustration, but it didn't hide the rejection in her deep brown eyes.

"I don't want to take advantage of you," he murmured. Well, he did. Desperately. But he wouldn't. If this war were over he'd marry Moira. He'd meant what he said the night they'd met, but this war wasn't even close to being over.

"Have you considered that I might like you to?"

"Would you care to repeat that?" His head buzzed with arousal and disbelief.

She held his gaze. "Perhaps, I'd like it if you did...if you took advantage of me."

She was serious.

"I might not survive." The thought of never seeing her again twisted his gut. "I want you to be taken care of...to marry." The thought of another man kissing her, loving her made him want to vomit.

Her fingers rose to the bodice of her dress and toyed with the buttons. "I don't want to be taken care of." She slid the glass disc through the hole, baring more of her creamy skin. "I don't want to marry." She unfastened another closure, her trembling fingers belying her composed demeanour. Dropping her gaze to the floor, she slipped the bodice off, letting the fabric hang limply over her hips. "I just want you."

Her pale skin shone in the sputtering candlelight. David had to shove his hands deep into his pockets. It was the only thing he could think to do to keep from touching her.

It didn't work.

His hands slipped free and he reached for her, dragging her against him. Barely able to believe he was holding a near-naked Moira in his arms, he slid his palms over the bare, soft skin of her back and urged her closer, kissing her like he'd wanted to since they'd met. Hard and deep, he plundered her mouth. She responded in kind, opening for him and kissing him thoroughly. She melted against him, a shuddering moan slipping from her lips as her mound came into contact with his rapidly hardening cock.

That small, strangled sound hit him like a bullet, and he jerked against her like untried schoolboy. He couldn't remember the last time he'd been so frantic with need. As he left her mouth to trace the gentle curve of her jaw with his lips, she tightened her fingers in his hair. The rasp of her breath and the scrape of her nails had his muscles quivering as he fought to hold himself in check.

She drew a shaky breath as he trailed down the side of her neck and over the curve of her shoulder, nipping at her skin before soothing with his lips. Tilting her head back, she offered herself to him. Unable to deny such a gift, he cupped the weight of her taut breasts in his hands. Her nipples pushed against the fabric of her bra, and she groaned as he palmed them. He'd never heard a more beautiful sound.

Eyes bright with desire and determination, she lifted her hands to his neck and began loosening his tie then made quick work of his buttons. Shrugging out of his shirt, he let it fall behind him as Moira yanked his undershirt from his waistband, her cool fingertips skimming over his stomach. "I want to touch you," she whispered as she stripped the shirt over his head.

The melodic lilt in her voice made him crazy. The touch of her hands—the taste of her lips made him crazy, too. Hell, everything about this woman made him crazy. For a moment, he closed his eyes, loving the sensation of her hands caressing his chest—tentative at first then growing bolder with every touch.

Opening his eyes, he gazed at her. Her teeth sank into her lower lip as she studied the bulge in his pants. Of course, the longer she stared at him, the bigger it grew. Occasionally, her fingers would skim over his waistband. He wanted to feel them wrapped around his cock, stroking him. Even more than that, he wanted to feel her mouth drawing on him and the wet clasp of her pussy as he drove inside her. But he wouldn't rush her.

Sliding his fingers into her long, dark hair, he angled her head for another kiss. He sucked her bottom lip into his mouth. This was heaven. This was what he'd longed for since he'd first seen her. Her hands settled at his waist as he soothed the spot he'd bitten with a sweep of his tongue. Laying her back against the cotton sacking, he slowly slipped her bra straps off her shoulders and unhooking it, bared her gorgeous breasts. She looked away, a blush colouring her cheeks.

"So beautiful," he murmured as he lay down beside her, rolling a tight, pink tip between his thumb and fingers, loving the way she arched into his touch. While he continued to torment one nipple, he drew the other into his mouth and sucked, flicking his tongue across the pebbled flesh.

On a moan, she grabbed him and held his head to her breast, keeping him where she wanted him. Complying, he stroked the bare skin of her stomach as his hand travelled downward and grazed her pussy through the skirt of her dress. She jerked as if burned, but she sighed his name, a long heated breath against the top of his head.

His cock throbbed, pushing against the buttons of his fatigue pants. He'd have grooves in his flesh if he didn't get inside her soon. But he'd rather have grooves than regrets, and he'd regret not making love to Moira as long as possible. With the bombs still falling and the likelihood of him joining the rest of the troops in France, who knew when they'd have another chance.

* * * *

Moira squirmed against David as the longing in her belly spread lower while he drew on her aching nipple. She'd never felt anything like the bliss of the wet heat of his mouth at her breast. She should be scandalised at his attentions. Instead, she trembled beneath his hands and lips. His touch stole her breath and her will.

As much pleasure as he gave, a restless need grew within her. She pulled him closer, loving the rub of the tight muscular planes of his body against her breasts. Needing the comfort of his nearness she closed her eyes and gave herself fully to his embrace. Explosions continued to shake the earth as well as her sense of security. She wanted more than comfort. She wanted him. Damn the consequences, she wanted to know how it felt to have his body pinning her to the ground. To know the sensation of him moving within her.

Moira sighed and pulled David closer. Between the sensation of his mouth at her nipple and his fingers dancing over her stocking clad legs as he inched her skirt higher it was nearly impossible to think. The stroke of his calloused fingertips against the bare skin at the top of her stocking sent quivers through her womb. She'd never allowed another man to take the liberties she'd offered so freely to David, nor could she imagine doing so, but with him, it felt right.

He brushed his thumb over the inside of her thigh, and his sharp intake of breath trembled through her as if it were her own. With tender whispers, he slipped his fingers between the silk and her skin and unhooked the garter that held up her stocking. His hand radiated heat as he cupped her bottom urging her into the press of his groin. A sweet ache spread through her and she wanted more — more of the restless need, more of his drugging kisses — just more of David. She tugged at her dress where it bunched between them. There were too many layers of fabric keeping them apart.

Releasing her for what felt like a year, he helped her skim the dress over her head. She laid back and closed her eyes, unable to bear his scrutiny. She knew she didn't compare to the beautiful blonde American women she'd seen in photographs. Forcing herself to look at him, she caught her breath. He looked at her like she was the most beautiful woman he'd ever seen. She knew better, but knowing didn't douse the pleasure she felt at his appreciation.

Desire thrummed through her blood at his hungry expression. As he took in her near naked form, his eyes had brightened in the dim light. They were the blue of a flame — a flame that was about to consume her. She shivered despite the heat bounding between them.

"Moira," he breathed.

She loved the sound of his voice, deep and rich, his American accent making it sound almost exotic. Frowning, she realised that she might be growing to love everything about this man. She'd have a broken heart before this was over, but she'd known that as soon as their gazes had met.

Almost reverently, he stroked her hip then dragged his fingertip along the crease where her thigh met her torso, slipping beneath the fabric of her underwear. She trembled as he drew closer to her core. A cry escaped her lips as he cupped her mound. She arched into his hand wanting more than this scant caress. As if he knew what she was thinking, he slipped his hand inside her underwear and dragged his finger through her moist folds. Dear God, had anything ever felt as good as his touch?

"You're so wet," he murmured.

Shamed heat flushed her cheeks and she glanced away.

"Don't be embarrassed." Withdrawing his hand from her panties, he lifted her hand and placed it on his erection. "It just means that you want me as much as I want you."

He throbbed beneath her palm. His arousal felt huge and seemed to be getting bigger by the moment. A tendril of fear snaked through her core as her fingers squeezed him through his trousers. He swallowed hard and his expression grew more ravenous, so she repeated the action. This time, his eyes closed briefly and he expelled a harsh breath through his nose.

"I want you so badly, but if you're not sure..."

"I'm sure."

She didn't miss the expression of relief that spread across his face. Gently moving her hand, he shifted to his knees as he finished unhooking and removed her garter belt. He placed her foot on his thigh and caressed the length of her leg as he slid his fingers up to catch the top of her stocking and drag it down. Repeating the action, he stripped her other leg.

She moved to pull off her panties, but he stilled her hands. "Let me."

Yielding to his quiet command, her hands fell limply to her sides. His face was a mask of fierce concentration as he bared her completely. Her belly tremored under his heated gaze as violently as the earth shook under the falling bombs.

"You're so beautiful," he breathed as he gazed down at her.

Desire darkened his eyes. They pulled at her like the tide and she wanted to lose herself in it. She wanted to lose herself in him. He made the terror and uncertainty of the war seem less overwhelming.

David leaned over her, caging her between his outstretched arms. She skimmed her hands over the broad expanse of his shoulders before raking her fingertips through the light sprinkling of hair over his chest. Curious, she followed the trail until it disappeared into his trousers. She loved the way his stomach quivered as she stroked him. It seemed that he was nearly as affected by her touch as she was by his. Tugging at the top button of his waistband she freed it from the closure.

Nervous anticipation fluttered madly through her stomach as she released the next button. It grew more intense with each subsequent fastener. Finally, the last button was undone and his erection sprung into her waiting hand. With shaking hands, she explored the smooth, silky steel, tracing each vein and ridge until she realised David's fists were clenched at his sides and he'd been gritting his teeth.

She snatched her hands away. "Am I hurting you?"

"No." He shook his head. "It just feels so good to have you touching me."

"Oh." She reached out to touch him again, but he caught her hands.

"I'm too close," he murmured, bringing her hands briefly to his lips. "Lay back." Lowering his head, he claimed her lips, delving deep and tasting her. He settled his weight atop her, his hips between her spread thighs.

Locking her arms around his neck, she urged him forward.

He raised his head and gazed at her. "Not yet."

Kissing her, he lured away her confusion until the only thing that existed was the caress of his lips and taste of his mouth. He slid his hand up her ribcage and moulded her breast, twisting and plucking at her nipple as she writhed against him. Barely cognizant of the attack outside, she lost herself in the feel of his warm flesh under her fingers and the comforting press of his body against hers.

His touch dulled the noise of the falling bombs but did nothing to quiet the sound of her pounding heart. For a brief moment, she questioned her sanity, lying naked in the arms of a virtual stranger, but when she looked into David's eyes, the worry faded along with her uncertainty. Nothing mattered but the places where their bodies touched.

David trailed his lips along her jaw to her neck and over the swell of her breasts. Drawing one nipple then the other into his mouth, he suckled on her, drawing needy moans from her as she drove her fingers through his hair. She'd never felt anything like the sensations he roused inside her. She wanted more, greedily arching her back, desperate for more of his sensitising touch.

As he continued to nip and draw on her aching nipples, he trailed his fingers downward, over her belly do dip between her moistened folds.

"Please, David...I need you inside me," she whispered, pushing her hips upward into his pleasuring hand.

He raised his head and stared into his flame blue eyes. "I want to taste you first."

"But you..."

He slipped two fingers deep inside her sheath, and she lost the ability to do more than groan.

Thrusting in and out of her, he laid a trail of kisses down her stomach to her mound. "I want to feel you come against my mouth," he murmured against the inside of her thigh.

Her stomach rippled in nervous response to the nearness of his mouth to her pussy. Gently withdrawing, he spread her wide before dragging his tongue through her gathering moisture. She'd never felt anything like it. Dear God, she wanted more. She *needed* more. David seemed to understand her strangled cry and responded by repeating his action.

With the tip of his tongue, he circled the swollen bit of flesh between her legs and returned his fingers to her clutching body. Moira trembled as she held his head in place with her hands. She wanted him pressing her into the earth, his cock filling her, but she didn't want him to stop what he was doing. As her hips rocked in quickening rhythm to his ministrations, she realised she didn't have a choice. Her body would follow wherever he led.

The sharp scent of her arousal permeated the dimly lit wine cellar as desire clawed at her, desperate for release. She writhed on their makeshift bed as his fingers filled her over and over and her juices covered his hand.

Lapping at her, he groaned. "You taste so good."

His words set off tremors that vibrated along her thighs, and her breath stalled in her chest. He slid his hands beneath her bottom to fit her more snugly to his mouth, and her body tightened like a rope pulled too taut. Sensation raced through her to centre in her womb as his thumbs played over her slick skin. Without warning, he sucked her engorged clit between his lips, his teeth scraping across the needy flesh.

The restless tension that had claimed her shattered, sending wave after wave of release flooding her body. Convulsing, she thrust her hips into David's face as he continued to draw on her as if he needed the taste of her to survive. Lights sparkled behind her closed lids as the tremors finally ebbed and faded leaving her sated.

Chapter Three

David finally lifted his head and met Moira's heavy-lidded gaze. She'd propped herself up on her elbows and watched him in the sputtering candlelight. He'd never tire of her — the taste of her sweet flesh, her throaty cries as she climaxed, the sound of his name falling from her lips. Everything about her excited him. More importantly, she filled something inside him he hadn't even realised had been empty.

Shifting, she sat up, drew him to his knees and palmed his aching cock. Absently, he thrust into her hand. He couldn't believe he'd managed to keep from coming as she'd found her release. He'd never seen anything more beautiful.

Now, holding his gaze, she caressed the length of his shaft, stopping to smear the drop of fluid that had leaked from the slit. With a secretive smile, she bent and swirled her tongue around the aching head before taking the tip into her mouth and sucking. Hard.

"Stop," he snapped, his hand tangled in the hair at the nape of her neck. He was too damn close to let her continue with her innocently erotic actions. Cupping her face, he kissed her in an attempt to soothe the wounded look in her eyes. Drawing back, he stared at her. "Please Moira, let me love you properly."

Urging her back against the floor, he finished stripping off his pants and boots then covered her with his body. He settled between her spread thighs, the tip of his cock grazing the sweet, wet heat of her pussy. His cock jerked. With more restraint than he thought he possessed he resisted the need to bury himself inside her warmth.

She smoothed her hand over his neck and shoulder. "Love me."

Nudging her thighs further apart, he lodged himself at her opening and pushed gently. She stiffened beneath him as he parted the untried tissues. "Do you want me to stop?"he gritted.

She shook her head and grasped his ass, pulling him forward.

He tried to hold back, but her tight, liquid passage proved irresistible. He shoved past the thin barrier until he was embedded so deeply, he couldn't move any further. Wincing, Moira trembled in his arms and he pulled her closer, guilt clogging his throat. "I'm so sorry. I didn't want to hurt you. I'm so sorry."

She pressed kisses over his shoulder and neck. "It's okay. I wanted this. I wanted you."

He kissed the tears from the corners of her eyes. "It gets better."

A small smile curved her full lips. "Show me."

David withdrew slowly before working his way back through her tender folds, watching her face for signs of discomfort. His muscles shook with his restraint as he kept his pace painstakingly measured—achingly slow. He sighed as she relaxed, tugging him closer, taking him deeper.

Her hips lifted to meet his, and small, needy sounds escaped her parted lips with each thrust. "I need more," she panted.

Slipping his arm around her waist, he urged her to wrap her legs around his waist. He groaned. The angle of contact changed and her satiny flesh clasped his cock even tighter. This was heaven—*she* was heaven. As long as he held her in his arms he could forget all of the ugliness he'd seen since the war had begun. Her lips opening beneath his chased away everything but Moira and this moment.

Her whispered encouragement pushed him harder and faster and he lost himself to the sensation of pounding into her eager body. Her fingernails scored his back as he pushed her closer to the edge. Meeting him thrust for desperate thrust, she stiffened and clamped down on his throbbing cock as her climax slammed into her. Her internal muscles shuddered and rippled, milking him until his balls tightened and he exploded within her. Panting, he gathered her closer, breathing in her sweet scent. God he wished this war was over. He wanted to fall asleep with her in his arms and wake up with her every morning.

Easing from her body, he tucked her into his side and dragged their discarded clothing over the top of them for warmth. The shelling above had stopped at some point, and now an eerie quiet had fallen. The only discernable noises were the sounds of their slowing breathing and the distant wail of an ambulance. As much as he wanted to stay down here with her, he knew he needed to leave the sanctuary of the wine cellar and offer assistance.

A quiet sigh escaped Moira and he leaned over and smoothed the hair from her face.

"What is it?" he asked.

She rolled her to her back and traced his features with her fingertip. "I hate the thought of leaving this place, but we should probably go and see what's left of the city." She swallowed hard. "And the people."

His stomach pitched as a thought occurred to him "We should check on your family."

She shook her head. "They're further north in Pengam. There's nothing there worth bombing. But I would like to check on my friends and the family I work for."

They dressed in near silence. There was so much he didn't know about her, but none of that mattered. He knew enough. He knew they were meant to be together. He just hoped she realised that too.

He glanced at Moira. Almost shyly, she pulled on her stockings. His cock hardened again as he watched the black slide of silk cover her legs, but he tried to force his desire away. As if she felt his eyes on her, she met his gaze. The desire he'd managed to tame roared back to life. The garter strap fell from her fingers and, she stood there wearing nothing but panties and half-hooked stockings.

"I love the way you look at me," she breathed as he crossed the tiny space between them.

He cupped the weight of her full breasts, brushing his thumbs across her nipples. "How do I look at you?"

A breath rattled through her as he drew a pebbled peak into his mouth, nibbling and sucking at it. "Like...like I'm the most beautiful woman in the world."

He released her breast and looked into her eyes. "You are."

She lifted her mouth to him, and he couldn't resist. Damn him, he should be out there searching for survivors, but instead, he had her pinned to a support beam while he devoured her lips.

Taking his hands, she placed them on her breasts. "Please, David..."

Palming them, he pushed his thigh between hers and she rocked against him.

"I need you again," she moaned.

He slipped his hand inside her panties and found her clit. She arched against him on a groan and began fumbling at the waistband of his pants.

"I need all of you," she whispered, shoving his pants over his hips.

As if he'd deny her. He pulled aside the crotch of her panties and poised the head of his cock at her slick entrance. Holding her steady, he filled her completely as she locked her legs at the small of his back. He couldn't believe he was ready for her again. He suspected it would always be this way between them. God willing, they'd have the chance to find out.

Wrapping his arms around her, he protected her delicate back from the wooden beam as he rocked into her, filling her over and over. Her breathless cries spurred him on as he thrust harder. He slipped a hand between them and plucked at her clit, rhythmically squeezing it between his thumb and forefinger. Her nipples jutted out and he drew one into his mouth sucking hard and gently scraping his teeth across it until she stiffened on a scream, her cream flooding around his cock.

Black spots floated in front of his eyes as a tingle started at the base of his spine and radiated outward. He emptied himself into her in hot shuddering gushes as she continued to milk his cock, taking everything he had to give.

He held her as their breathing quieted before finally letting her slip to her feet. A self-conscious smile curved her lips as she smoothed a shaking hand over her hair. "I guess we should probably hurry. I'm sorry I slowed us down."

He pulled her into his arms. "Don't be sorry. There's nowhere else I'd rather be."

She traced the line of his jaw. "You fancy musty wine cellars, then?

He laughed and brushed a tender kiss across her lips. "I fancy you."

* * * *

Moira paced in front of the dance hall on Wood Street. Miraculously, it had escaped damage during last week's raid. The nearby buildings weren't as lucky. All told, forty-six people had died in the bombing. After she and David had left the shelter, they'd helped move the injured to the hospital. Outside the hospital, they'd run into one of his fellow soldiers who'd been looking for him. Despite their weekend pass, they were required to report back to camp immediately, so David had kissed her goodbye, promising he'd be back.

Nine days later and she still hadn't heard from him. She wanted to believe she'd meant more to him than a quick tumble. God knew she was all but in love with him, but the longer she went without hearing from him, the more she worried she'd been wrong about him.

Worry tightened her middle as she pushed the thought away. What if something happened to him? How would she ever know? She sincerely doubted his captain would bother to search her out to tell her the news. Was it possible he'd been shipped out already? He wouldn't leave without saying goodbye. At least, she didn't think he would. Blinking back the sting of tears, she turned towards the sound of footsteps descending the concrete stairs of the dance hall. Bethan and a man Moira didn't recognise.

"Moira," her friend called. "This is Lieutenant Portko, he's been looking all over for you.

Her stomach fell to the sidewalk as she turned to face the man. "I'm Moira. How can I help you?"

The officer offered her a grim smile and removed a bulky envelope from the inside pocket of his jacket. "I promised a young man I'd find you and give you this." He laid the envelope in Moira's outstretched hand and she closed her fingers around it.

"Is he..." She couldn't force the remainder of the question past her throat as she stared at the man.

"In France," the man finished, gruffly.

Silently saying a prayer for David's safety, she nodded and blinked back tears. From a distance, she heard Bethan and the lieutenant talking as she sank onto the step. The cold seeped through the thin fabric of her skirt, chilling her as she carefully opened the envelope.

Inside, was David's watch, wrapped in a note. Smoothing the paper over her knees, she squinted at his sloppy handwriting.

Dearest Moira,

I'm sorry I had to leave without saying goodbye, but I was hoping you'd hold this for me. I'll come for you as soon as I'm able. I miss you like mad.

All my love,
David

Relief raced through her body and she sagged against the railing. He hadn't forgotten her.

Chapter Four

Moira stood with her back to the brisk April breeze in the backyard of the home where she worked. Shaking out the bed sheet, she pinned it to the clothesline. Her skirt caught in the breeze and David's watch bumped against her thigh, a comforting weight in her pocket. It was stupid to continue to carry it around after all this time. It had been almost two years since she'd seen him and six months since she'd heard from him. The war had ended in December, so where was he?

She was terrified something had happened to him. Hundreds of thousands of men had died in this war. Swallowing past the lump that clogged her throat whenever she thought of David, she realised she might never know what happened to him. There was also the nagging worry that he'd found someone else. After all, they'd only been together once, and they'd had so little time together. Her hands clenched on the pillow case she was hanging and tears filled her eyes. A fool. That's what she was. She'd been nothing more than a pleasant distraction.

Now that the fighting had stopped, the neighbourhood was gradually resuming its normal activity. The rumble of a slow moving vehicle filled the quiet spring air as the driver rounded the corner. A delivery truck, no doubt. However, instead of continuing up the street to the restaurant, it stopped in front of the house. Tossing the clothes pins back into the basket, she pushed aside the hanging linens and rounded the side of the building. It wasn't a delivery truck, but a jeep. A military jeep.

Her heart leapt into her throat as a man exited from the passenger side. *David.* She'd dreamed of seeing him again—more times than she could count. She wasn't even sure she wasn't imagining him now. She wanted to believe this was real—to go to him, but shock kept her rooted to the spot. Shock and fear. It was entirely possible he'd only come to retrieve his watch. And say goodbye. Steeling herself against the possibility, she waited.

David paused. For months he'd ached for this woman, and now she stood there—just staring at him, velvet brown eyes wide with worry. Had she moved on to someone else? When he'd questioned nearly everyone in the city of Cardiff as to her whereabouts, he'd never bothered to find out if she'd married. Even if she hadn't, perhaps she'd decided he hadn't been worth waiting for.

Ignoring the pain of his injury, he waved away the driver. Limping, he forced one foot in front of the other and pushed open the garden gate. As if freed from a spell, she darted across the yard and threw herself into his arms.

He wrapped his arms around her and pressed her to his body, unwilling to let the smallest of spaces between them. Lifting her face, he covered her lips and delved into her mouth like he'd wanted to for so long. She melted against him, driving her fingers through his hair, her need evident in her kiss. God, this was where he needed to be. Warm moisture dampened his cheeks, and he realised she was crying. He pulled back and brushed away her tears. "Moira, love, what's this?"

Swallowing hard, she dashed her hand across her eyes. "I was so afraid that something had happened to you...and when I didn't get any responses from you, I thought..." Unable to finish, she buried her face in his chest.

He gestured to his leg. "I've been bounced from one field hospital to another. I never got your letters."

She lifted her head, her eyes clouded with worry. "What happened?"

He shrugged. "Lucky shot."

"You should be sitting down," she scolded, tugging his arm. "Come with me. You need to rest."

Looking into her eyes, he wrapped his arms around her and refused to let her move. "I've got everything I need right here."

She opened her mouth, but he laid his finger across her full lips. "Unless you're about to tell me that you want me to leave, stop talking and kiss me."

Frowning, she slapped his shoulder. "Of course I don't want you to leave!"

He nuzzled her neck, pushing aside the collar of her dress with his lips. "That's good, since I wasn't planning on going anywhere."

A tremor shivered through her as he dragged open-mouthed kisses up the side of her neck sinking his teeth into her earlobe. Her nipples peaked, pressing into his chest. He sighed as he took her mouth in a hungry kiss. The sweet taste of her exploded across his tongue and he groaned as he delved deeper.

He'd missed the sensation of her in his arms more than he could express. His hand slid up her ribcage and he brushed his thumb across a pebbled nipple, loving her responsive nature. Hell, what *didn't* he love about her? They'd discovered so much more about each other through their letters, and he'd learned he'd been right the first time he'd seen her. She was the woman he was going to marry. She was the woman he loved.

He pulled her closer, shifting when something dug into his thigh brushing the wound. Dismissing the pain, he cupped her breast, moulding it and reacquainting himself with the glory of her body. Breathless, he broke the kiss. "Do you have any idea how much I've missed you?"

She gazed at him with such tenderness, his chest ached. "I think I do," she murmured, her eyes bright with tears. Wrapping her arms around his neck, she backed against the side of the house and pulled him with her.

Something in her pocket again pressed against his injury. Wincing, he plucked at her skirt. "I think you should take whatever this is out of your pocket, or better yet, just take off your dress."

Laughing, she reached into her pocket and withdrew his watch. "I ought to give this back to you since it's causing so much trouble."

He trailed his fingertip along her neckline. "I'm not sure I can accept it."

"I don't understand." Her brow furrowed in confusion.

"I'd be willing to trade you for it." Try as he might, he couldn't hide his smile as he reached into his jacket pocket for the tiny box he'd been carrying around since he'd returned to Britain. Opening the latch, he pulled the ring from the satin cushion and closed his fingers around it before tugging his hand from the pocket.

"Have you gone daft? It's *your* wristwatch."

She pressed the timepiece into his hand. "Honestly David, you'd think you had a head wound rather than a leg injury."

"Shall I assume that since you're returning this that you'll accept my trade sight unseen?"

Seemingly bewildered, she pursed her lips and stared at him for a long moment. "What are you on about?"

Opening her fingers, he laid the ring on her palm. "A watch for a wedding ring." He lifted her chin to stare into her wide eyes. "Marry me, Moira. Please."

Her gaze darted between his face and her palm and a flash of worry seared his gut. Perhaps he should have waited until she'd had more time to readjust to his return. Perhaps he should have waited until he could afford a better ring. This one wasn't nearly as grand as she deserved.

She slowly shook her head. "I don't need a ring, you silly man." Her voice broke and she had to clear her throat to continue. "I just need you."

His fear receded and was quickly replaced by growing joy. "Is that a yes?"

She nodded. He plucked the ring from her hand and slipped it on her finger. The tiny diamonds and sapphires sparkled in the afternoon light, but their beauty paled in comparison to Moira.

"I love you," she whispered, her voice thick with tears.

"And I love you."

A watery smile curved her lips and she pulled him towards the door. "Show me."

He glanced pointedly at the house. "Is there anyone else home?" From what he'd heard while he was searching for her, she worked as domestic help for a prominent family. He doubted her employers would appreciate returning home to find them in bed.

"They're in Scotland — on vacation," she said as she opened the door and pulled him in into the kitchen, locking the door behind them.

"Good." Settling his hands at her waist, he backed her against the kitchen counter. "When are they due back?"

"Next week some time." Breathless, she smoothed her hands over his chest.

"I might be ready to let you out of bed by then."

Her breath caught, and he felt it in his hardening cock as he trailed his lips over her neck. "For a while," he added as he took her lips again. Her sweet scent nearly brought him to his knees.

He drove his hands through her hair, angling her head to delve more deeply into her mouth. The memory of her taste, her satiny skin, the wet clasp of her body — they'd given him comfort in the cold, muddy foxholes. Knowing that someday she'd be in his arms again had given him the strength to push through the frozen winters and past his fallen comrades.

So grateful to have her in his arms again, he crushed her to him. Her lips parted for him as she eagerly welcomed his tongue. Her arms slid around him, her fingertips digging into his shoulders as she silently demanded more. God knew he was more than ready to give her what she wanted.

With frantic motions, she tugged at his shirt, pulling it from the waistband of his pants and smoothing her hands over his stomach. His cock throbbed painfully. It had been too damn long, and he was beginning to doubt he'd last more than a few thrusts. She made quick work of his buttons, but he grabbed her hands and pinned them to the cupboards above her head.

Keeping her immobilized, he nibbled at her pouting lower lip. "As much as I want you," he murmured between tastes of her mouth, "I have to insist on a bed, this time."

Her beautiful brown eyes clouded and her brow furrowed as she pulled her wrists from his loose grasp. "Your leg! I'm so sorry. You should already be lying down."

She took his hand and led him down the hall into a small sunny bedroom off the kitchen. Worry pulled her lips into a frown as she stood by the side of a small narrow bed. "Lie down, please. I'll get you some water. Do you need some aspirin?"

"No." Scooping her into his arms, he deposited her into the centre of the bed. David pinned her to the mattress, caging her with his arms. "I don't give a damn about my leg. This is for you."

Her lips parted, echoing the confusion that showed in her eyes. Taking advantage of her open mouth, he kissed her. Sweeping inside, he lost himself in her sweetness as she wrapped her arms around his neck and drew him closer.

When he finally broke the kiss and lifted his head, she stared into his eyes.

"I'm not sure I understand." Shifting against his hardened cock, she smiled. "I'm also not sure I care."

Happier than he could ever remember being, he smoothed the hair back from her face. "The bed is for you."

Before she could speak, he laid his finger across her lips. "Your first time was on a pile of empty flour sacks in a bombed out wine cellar."

Scowling, she bit his finger. "So?"

He removed his hand and placed it at her waist. "The second time was up against a splintery support beam." He slid his hand upward to rest under the curve of her breast.

"Did you hear me complaining?" she asked.

One by one, he popped open the buttons on her dress until he'd exposed the creamy skin of her breasts. The bra had to go. Reaching around her back, he unhooked the contraption and slid his hand under the fabric and he cupped the full, firm mound. He kneaded her flesh and her nipple hardened instantly beneath his palm. Moira arched into his hand as a strangled moan escaped her lips.

"Of course," she added breathlessly, "I'm not complaining now, either." She shoved his shirt off his shoulders and spread heated kisses everywhere she could reach. "Too many clothes," she said, between caresses.

"I thought you weren't complaining." He laughed as she narrowed her eyes at him.

"Get your clothes off, soldier."

"Ladies first." He slid his hand up her bare leg, dragging her skirt as he went. He hooked his fingers in her panties and pulled them down before cupping her mound.

Moira bit back a groan as David's fingers swept through her damp heat and she pushed against him. Dear God, it felt good to have his hands on her again. It had been far too long and she needed so much more than what he was giving her. She wanted his tightly leashed passion, and she wanted it now. They had plenty of time later for slow and gentle.

Struggling to a sitting position, she kicked off her shoes and yanked off the remainder of her clothing while he stood and did the same. She caught her breath at the red, puckered scar that marred his leg. Swallowing hard, she pushed back the lump that clogged her throat and scooted to the edge of the bed. She bent and placed tender kisses around the wound.

"You could have been killed," she choked out.

He lifted her chin and stared into her eyes. "Not when I knew you were waiting for me."

Her heart stuttered at the intensity in his voice. Blinking back a flood of happy tears, she teased, "You Americans certainly know how to woo a girl."

He laughed, love and desire lighting his brilliant blue eyes. Giving her a playful shove, he covered her with his body, his erection prodding at her opening. "We certainly do."

He dragged the head of his cock through the cream flooding her pussy. Just as quickly the playful atmosphere vanished, leaving them with nothing but desperation.

"Don't tease," she breathed. "I need you."

"No more teasing," he agreed and drove inside her.

She cried out as his thick heat filled her, stretched her. It had been so long. Finally. *Finally* he was home. He was where he belonged.

David stopped moving, frozen as if in pain. Slowly, he opened his eyes. "You feel so good," he grated. "But I don't want to move. I want this to be good for you, too."

She pushed her hips against his, loving the sensation of their joined bodies. "Love me, now," she murmured, thrusting against him again.

"Two years ago...now...for the rest of our lives," he replied through gritted teeth.

Moira kissed him, tumbling over the edge of forever with him. They truly did have the rest of their lives. War had brought so much devastation, but their love had survived and risen...from the ruins.

About the Authors

Aliyah Burke

Aliyah Burke lives on the East Coast with her husband. They have two dogs and a cat. A Navy wife, she enjoys hearing from her readers. If you visit her website, please don't forget to sign the guest book.

Jennah Sharpe

Jennah Sharpe is an author, mother and traveller who can be easily seduced by mint chocolate. Her imagination often keeps her up at night but it certainly makes for an entertaining life. She lives in Canada with her soul mate and two young children.

SL Majors

SL Majors enjoys living on the edge. She pens stories to tantalise and arouse, maybe shock and, hopefully, to make you think.

From her earliest years exploring England and Wales (and finding out early what nettles are!), she's learnt that things aren't always as they seem. She hopes to capture that in her stories.

She encourages you to delight in life and the unexpected, embracing each experience. It's her greatest hope that at the end of her stories, you'll say, "What if?"

Bronwyn Green

I live in Michigan with my wonderful husband, two amazing sons and seven somewhat psychotic cats.

When not tormenting my characters, I can usually be found helping with reading, writing and art projects in my sons' classrooms as well as providing child care and tutoring for several daycare children.

Besides writing, I also enjoy reading, knitting, sewing, cross stitching, pottery, drawing, jewellery making – basically anything that helps me avoid cooking and cleaning.

The authors love to hear from readers. You can find their contact information, website details and author profile pages at http://www.total-e-bound.com

Total-e-Bound Publishing

www.total-e-bound.com

Take a look at our exciting range of literagasmic™
erotic romance titles and discover pure quality
at Total-E-Bound.